MW01422676

FIC Johns

Johnson, S.
An American haunting.

CAMBRIDGE
PUBLIC LIBRARY
THE LIBRARY
& GALLERY

✓

PRICE: $34.95 (3556/qsm)

JAN 1 1 2005

AN AMERICAN HAUNTING

AN AMERICAN HAUNTING

Scott A. Johnson

HH
HARBOR
HOUSE
AUGUSTA

AN AMERICAN HAUNTING
By Scott A. Johnson
A Harbor House Book/2004

Copyright 2004 by Scott A. Johnson

All rights reserved. No part of this book may be reproduced or transmitted in any form or by any means, electronic or mechanical, including photocopying, recording, or by any information storage and retrieval system, without permission in writing from the publisher.

For information address:
    HARBOR HOUSE
    111 10TH STREET
    AUGUSTA, GEORGIA 30901

Jacket Design by Charles Bernard

Library of Congress Cataloging-in-Publication Data

Johnson, Scott A. (Scott Asburry), 1971-
An American haunting / by Scott A. Johnson.
p. cm.
ISBN 1-891799-11-8 (hardcover : alk. paper)
1. Haunted houses--Fiction. 2. Home ownership--Fiction. 3. Texas--Fiction. I. Title.
PS3610.O377A83 2004
813'.6--dc22

Printed in the United States of America
10 9 8 7 6 5 4 3 2 1

*This book is respectfully dedicated to my family,
especially Tabby, Anna and Zoe.
Thank you.*

PROLOGUE

MARIAN SCRAMBLED DOWN THE HALLWAY, her eyes wide, mouth frozen in a scream that would not come. As the lights flickered, she could only think to get out, get away before she too became a casualty. She'd lost sight of her husband, last seen sitting in a drunken stupor in the kitchen, screaming that he belonged to the house and it loved him more than her. The deafening roar that followed her like waves crashing on a beach made her dizzy, causing her to stumble as she ran. It seemed that the house was collapsing in upon itself, trying to catch her, as would hands trying to catch a cricket. The floorboards rattled and thumped, making her flight more perilous. Marian reached the front door only to find it would not open, stuck or held by an unseen force.

The room seemed to come alive around her, and she clutched at her hair, as though by pulling it out this hideous vision would go. Pictures fell from the walls, China cups leapt from their shelves, crashing into the door behind her. As one struck her knee, she fell to the floor, heaving sobs of pain and fear.

"Leave me alone!" she wailed to the house.

She felt the doorway twist and contort behind her. Nearly frozen with terror, she turned to see the door twist and bulge until an all-too-familiar face emerged. It was the face she'd seen beckoning her in the nightmares that began when she and her husband moved in, the same face she'd seen smiling at her in mirrors out of the corner of her eye. It was that cherubic face, twisted in hatred and evil, that now loomed before her, its mouth wide open in a guttural howl of defiance.

She felt her feet begin to kick and somehow got moving, this time toward the back door. The fireplace erupted, a gateway to hell. The plaster cracked as the house began to violently quake. She got through the hallway to the kitchen where her husband, no longer raving, stood smiling dementedly, the gleaming axe in his hand smiling back.

"I was wrong, you know," he said. His voice was barely above a whisper, but she could hear him plainly over the din. "It wants you too. We all want you. Stay with us!"

He lunged for her, barely an eyelash away from her delicate flesh. The axe whizzed past her, slicing the bodice of her gauze nightgown. She screamed and leaped for the door, swinging at her husband, connecting with his temple. He fell to the floor, dazed.

He looked at the axe as if seeing it for the first time and dropped it. "My God," he said softly.

Marian was clawing at the door, though it refused to open either. Her voice was raw from screaming and she could taste blood in the back of her throat, but the sound would not stop. She caught movement from the corner of her eye and whirled to see her husband, his face filled with rage, swing the axe high overhead. She screamed and closed her eyes as the deadly weapon began to fall. She heard the clank of metal on metal and opened her eyes. Steven had swung the axe and cut through the latch on the door. Now he was kicking with all his might to open it.

"Run!" he shouted as the door flew open. The house howled.

Marian stared, unable to comprehend what had just happened. Had he killed her and she not felt it? Had he missed and was going to try again? Was he again himself?

"Goddamit," he cried. "Get up! Get out of here!"

He grabbed her roughly by the arm and slung her through the open doorway, sending her sprawling across the terra-cotta tile outside. She watched in horror as inky black tendrils embraced him as a lover. The look on his face said fear, abandonment, enslavement. With a howl, the door to the house slammed shut, and Marian was left alone, sobbing gently on the tile, surrounded by the rotting remains of what was once her garden.

CHAPTER 1

THE OLD HOUSE LAY DORMANT behind its wrought-iron gates, quietly awaiting new tenants. It stood in the historic district of San Marcos on an out-of-the-way street as if unrecognized by the other, more prestigious houses.

It was not so different from them, with its long white pillars and gently sloping front yard. Its porch was broad and inviting, and its heavy wooden door seemed to welcome any and all visitors. The trees in its yard, though badly needing a trim, were really quite beautiful, and the flowerbeds, now overgrown with weeds, were at one time, to be sure, stunning.

The steps to the front door were not so steep as to be imposing, but just high enough to impart respect. Along one side of the house there was an open area, a place where previous occupants had planted a plum tree, and where the sun shone down and warmed the grass. The other side was a wide path to the back yard, what many considered to be the selling point of the house.

The wide terracotta patio and stone flowerbeds were beautiful, but it was the small cottage in the corner of the yard that seemed to fascinate prospective buyers. With its little shingled roof and door no taller than five feet in height, this little house was meant for the children that surely lived here once. A house in need of a family, that's what it was. But with no family to fill its halls with joy, it slept.

The neighboring houses, one a model of historic pride, the other a beauty fallen victim to neglect and ruin, seemed to stand as sentries, guarding their little stretch of street. They were the only three houses on this block. It was theirs. They were joined to the third by way of a stone wall which ran the front of all of their yards. Behind it, the houses rose high above the street, monuments of a time long passed.

The house was nearly seventy years old. It had seen all but the very dawn of San Marcos, which began over one hundred years ago as little more than a teacher's college in the Texas hill country. As its reputation grew, more students came and with them, prosperity. Though the population tripled for nine months out of every year, it had still managed to stay small and quiet. This was because the students went North or South, either way less than an hour's drive, to a sprawling metropolis, for their fun. At 10 p.m. this town rolled up its sidewalks and went to sleep.

The previous tenants of the old house, a nice married couple, had bought it with plans of modernizing it, a mixture of past and future. The neighbors were shocked when the renovation suddenly stopped and the house went up for sale. No one actually saw the couple leave, only the movers who packed up and moved the contents of the home. Rumors drifted that alcohol involved. Another speculated that adultery was at the heart of the hasty departure. Still more said the house simply did not like them. Whatever the case, the old house was now empty, waiting for someone to come breathe life back into its dull windows. Occasionally, neighbors sensed movement in the empty house, or heard noises, as the house waited, waited for a new family so it wouldn't be alone.

CHAPTER 2

"What did I tell you?" asked the man in the torn blue jeans and t-shirt to his companion, a shorter man with blond hair and a goatee.

"Jesus, Toby. This place is a dump," he replied, looking around the darkened living room. "Mom and Dad aren't going to go for this. There's too much work left to be done."

"You just don't see the potential," Toby replied, his grin never slipping for an instant. "Besides, you and I are going to be doing most of the work on it ourselves. Don't you think this place will be beautiful?"

It was hardly a word that came to mind when Gabe looked around the room. He saw floors that needed to be replaced, painting that needed to be done, and they hadn't even gotten past the front room.

"I think he's right!" said the all-too-chipper real estate agent. "And an old house like this never goes down in value!"

Gabe said nothing, just continued to walk around the living room. It *was* interesting, he'd give it that, with its high ceilings and transoms over the doorways. He passed into the next room, a long chamber with a bare bulb hanging from wires in the ceiling.

"Dining room?" he asked.

"I think so," said the agent, thumbing through the pages of her notebook. "Of course, you can use it for whatever you want..."

She went on to explain how this room could be used for this or that, but Gabe was not listening. He was surveying the room for potential trouble spots in construction. Also, he was cold. Not the kind of cold one feels when the room temperature is set too low, but the type one feels when they are being watched.

Now, as he glanced about the room with his brother and the sales agent chattering about potential improvements to be made with the house, he felt the house was surveying him as surely as he was it. Gabe continued walking along creaking floorboards and glanced into the side bedroom.

"This is an awfully narrow space for a bedroom, isn't it?"

"Well, the previous owners used it as an office, mainly because it connects to the workroom. Follow me." She led the way through the room to a bathroom and out the door on the other side. As he crossed the threshold to the room beyond, the cold he felt dissipated. "Now this section of the home is only twenty years old or so."

"Oh?" said Gabe, looking up.

"It was added on after the fire that claimed part of the back section of the house."

Toby whirled about. "Fire?" he asked, suddenly serious.

"A small house fire that happened when the dining area was a kitchen when the house was first built," she said with a dismissive wave. "That was a long time ago. If you'll follow me, I'll show you the rest of the house."

She led them through the large room to one of two doors on the opposite wall.

"That door," she said, pointing to the second door, "leads up to the garage and outside. This one leads to the kitchen."

The kitchen was unfinished, with bare sheet-rock walls and a concrete floor, temporary cabinets and power outlets with no covers on them.

"This kitchen is huge," beamed Toby. "Trish will love this!"

"Yeah," muttered Gabe. "When it's finished." He was still puzzling over the coldness that had disappeared. Whatever he felt, it was not in this section of the house either.

"Is this section new as well?" he asked.

"Yep," said the agent matter-of-factly. "In fact, if you look closely at the threshold that leads back into the dining area, you can see where the old house stops and the new one begins."

They followed her through the doorway back into the old section of the house. When he crossed the threshold, Gabe felt cold again. Whatever it was, it was limited to the older section. They went past a flight of stairs into the master bedroom.

"Now this is where the renovation stopped with the previous owners," she said. "If you look in the bathroom, you'll see what I mean."

To say the bathroom was large would be an understatement. It was longer than most of the bedrooms in the house. The areas that were new were evidenced by bare sheetrock walls, same as the kitchen. The previous owners had made closets, effectively separating the front and back half of the bathroom and masking the presence of a large hot-tub that sat in a raised platform off to one side.

"Who puts a hot-tub in their bathroom in Texas?" mused Toby.

"People who want to pay high air-conditioning bills?" joked Gabe.

They made their way back to the front of the house where the agent showed them the last bedroom, a medium-sized area with its own bathroom.

"Well," said the agent in an awkward attempt to wrap up the tour, "is there anything else?"

"Yeah," said Gabe intently. "Where do those stairs go?"

"Oh," she said hesitantly. "That's the unfinished basement."

"A basement in Texas?" asked Toby.

"It's not really a basement," said the agent with a forced laugh. "Most of the houses built when this one was are built on timbers, like legs. The builders just decided to enclose those timbers here."

"Can we see it?" asked Gabe.

"Feel free to go down there, if you like. I don't because it's not very clean and I have other appointments today." Gabe could tell she was being evasive. She smiled weakly. "Must keep up the company image, right?"

Toby and Gabe looked at one another and without a word, made for the stairs. At the bottom, they opened the door and peered into the dim room. It was unfinished, that was true, but it was evident by the ruined bar and the couches built into the wall that someone had, at one time, wanted to make it into an entertainment area. They walked around the room for a few moments before Toby spoke.

"So what do you think?"

Gabe was thoughtful. He wasn't one to rush into decisions. His parents had loaned him money from their retirement fund for the down payment on the house, and he wasn't keen on wasting their money. There was so much work to be done on this house, perhaps more than he could do without professional contractors. The labor was one thing, but the expense of such an undertaking was another entirely.

Still, there was something about this house that intrigued him. Perhaps it was the potential that his brother and the real-estate agent saw in it, potential he was beginning to see. Perhaps it was the location, close to both his work and his brother's house. More likely, it was the cold, the presence he felt. It was stronger here in the basement than anywhere else he'd been thus far. Something about it seemed, not malevolent, but more curious, and he wanted to find out more about it. At any rate, he would be unable to find a house of this caliber at this low of a price.

"I like it."

Toby grinned and clapped his hands together. "Yes! I knew it! I'll call Mom and Dad when I get home!"

"Here," said Gabe, lobbing his cellphone at his brother. "Use this."

Toby fumbled with the keypad and raised the phone to his ear.

"Mom? We found them a house! Yeah! It's got a lot of potential..."

Gabe wasn't listening to the rest of the conversation. He was looking around, searching for the hidden cause of this strange cold that seemed to work from inside his soul outward.

CHAPTER 3

Within a few days, their parents had driven down, agreed with Toby, and arranged for a transfer of funds for a down payment on the house. Days later, the house was theirs. It was decided Gabe and his family would assume the mortgage payments within a few months so his funds could be used to begin the arduous task of replacing rotted timbers, painting and making the place livable. It was a good arrangement for them, as they had recently filed bankruptcy and needed some time to get their financial footing back without worrying about rent. They looked upon the house and his parent's generocity as a God-send.

"This place is incredible," Trish said, looking around over the large cardboard box she was carrying. It was the first time she'd seen the house, knowing only it was in the historic district and that her husband said it needed some work. Behind her crept their oldest daughter, Lizzy.

"Mommy." She began most of her sentences this way. "This is where we're going to live?"

"Yes, honey," Trish sighed as she put the box down on the counter in the kitchen. "For a while anyway."

"Everything looks so old."

"That's because it is, sweetheart." It was Gabe walking in behind her, a large box under one arm and their youngest daughter, Shannon, in the other. "We're going to fix it up and make it like new again."

Lizzy looked around with a doubtful expression like only a ten-year-old girl can master.

"Tell you what," Trish said. "There are two more bedrooms in this house that haven't been claimed. Go pick one."

Lizzy ran further into the house with Shannon in tow. Gabe put the box down next to the wall.

"What do you think?" he asked.

"I love what I've seen. But there's a whole lot of work to be done."

"Yeah, I know," he sighed. "Wait'll you see the rest."

"Geez," huffed Toby as he struggled through the door with a large box. "You guys've got a lot of stuff."

Unloading the U-Haul trailer took very little time, and for now, they weren't going to unpack very much. There was no sense setting up their entire lives when they were going to have to shuffle things during construction. Only the boxes containing clothes, essentials, and the children's toys were to be opened. Memories and knickknacks were to stay packed, stored in the garage, waiting for a better time.

Lizzy, the oldest, had gotten the pick of the other two rooms and had chosen the larger one that faced the front of the house. Shannon, being only two, had little to say in the matter. So long as her toys were in a place she could get to them, she was happy.

By the time they were done, Lizzy's room contained four large boxes labeled "Lizzy's Stuff, DO NOT TOUCH" and only one box marked "LR- Clothes." Shannon's room was already a mess of toys and clothes as she had, in an unsupervised moment, gotten into both her boxes and pulled everything out. She sat playing with her baby dolls, singing to them softly in gibberish.

Gabe, Trish, Toby and his wife, Sarah, sat outside on the terra-cotta patio smoking, exhausted from the long day.

"This is going to be so cool," said Toby.

"Yeah," sighed Gabe. "It'll be nice to get the finances under control again."

"I meant the house."

"Oh... yeah... that too."

"If you ever get it finished," said Sarah. She never was one to keep her opinions to herself. "This house would be too much work for me. And besides, it feels creepy."

Trish looked up. "What do you mean, 'creepy'?"

"Didn't you feel like you were being watched the whole time we were unloading?"

"Honey," said Toby. "You're paranoid."

The back door opened and Shannon appeared, beaming with innocent joy.

"Hi honey!" called out Trish.

"Hi mommy! Wha doing?" Her language skills were progressing at a wonderful rate, with her learning new words every day. She waddled to her mother and raised her arms, her way of saying she wanted to be picked up. Trish took her onto her lap.

"What'cha got?" she asked, reaching for the dark object under her child's arm.

Shannon clutched the old rag doll tighter. "Bee-bee!" she said.

Trish knew every toy that both her daughters had. She knew which were their favorites and which were kept only because they were gifts. This was something she had not seen before. It was old, that was for sure. Its dark burlap face held shining blue buttons for eyes and a small string of red yarn where a mouth would be. From beneath the red gingham bandana on its head, black yarn escaped like little snakes. It wasn't that this little doll was unfamiliar to her that bothered Trish. It was that the simple white dress it wore was charred in some places.

"Where did you get this?" Shannon did not answer, only grinned and nuzzled the doll. "Honey, look at this."

"Hmmm... cute," he said. "It looks hand made."

"Yeah, but where did it come from? And why is it burned."

"I dunno."

Toby leaned in close. "It's a pickaninny doll. Probably left by the old owners."

Sarah looked at the doll and shivered. "It's creepy."

Toby rolled his eyes.

"Whatever it is," said Trish, "I don't like it."

"Mine!" said Shannon, jumping out of her mother's lap and running back into the house.

CHAPTER 4

SHANNON CLIMBED OUT OF HER LITTLE TODDLER BED and sat quietly on the floor of her room surrounded by boxes to be unpacked tomorrow, the dim illumination provided by her night-light casting strange and grotesque shadows on the walls. She'd played this game before, waking up in the still-darkened morning and playing before her mommy heard her and put her back to bed.

At two years old, she was already a bright little girl whose eyes hinted that she knew more than she let on. She clutched her empty bottle under one arm and rocked her arms back and forth as though listening to a cheery song.

Giggling, she watched the shadows on the walls and ceiling ebb and flow and concentrate into a single corner. She watched as the shadows came away from the wall and drifted like smoke across the room encircling her. The shadows flicked and tickled her and sounded like little bells and whispers as they played their game with the grinning toddler.

In their room, Trish drifted out of sleep, as she had done many nights, to the sounds from the monitor receiver, the transmitter for which was in Shannon's room. Only half-awake, she kicked the blankets off and slid her feet down to the cold wooden floor, which made her wince. She felt around with her toes until she located her slippers, giant stuffed mice her husband had bought for her, and rubbed her itchy eyes. In mid-yawn her stomach knotted and her heart froze. There were several voices coming from the monitor, not just her daughter's. Whispers, barely audible, hissed into her ears and panic began to creep into her mind. She violently shook her husband.

"Gabe," she half-whispered.

"Huh? Whazzat?"

"There's someone in this house!"

"No... Go back to sleep..."

"I hear voices from Shannon's room."

Gabe sat bolt upright, instantly wide awake, his face a mix of fear and anger. He listened for a moment, then, hearing the whispers, scrambled out of bed, taking with him an old pee-wee league baseball bat he kept under his side of the bed.

"Stay here," he said. "Get ready to call the police."

With his terrified wife sitting with her hand on the telephone, Gabe crept as quickly as he could across the dining room to his daughter's door. Was that movement he saw in the shadows through the transom above the door? He threw the door open, bat held high.

Shannon lay in her bed, her blankets pulled up snugly under her arms, playing with the little burlap doll and jabbering softly to herself.

"Hi Daddy!" she said brightly. "Wha doing?"

Gabe did not answer as he looked behind the doors and into the bathroom. Satisfied the room was empty, he looked at his youngest.

"Hi honey," he said quietly. "What're you doing awake?" He smiled at her.

"Paying."

"Playing with who, honey?"

Shannon looked up from her doll and pointed toward the corner of the room.

"What? Was someone there?" he asked.

She grinned and ducked her chin, her look that said: "I'm being cute."

He bent down and picked her up, bottle, doll, and all, and made one last look around the room before exiting, closing the door behind him. He made his way back to the room where Trish was waiting and found her still perched by the telephone, a look of panic and fear firmly etched on her face.

"There was no one there," he said, plopping Shannon on the bed next to her mother.

"Who was she playing with?"

"I don't know," he said. "She pointed at an empty corner." He pulled the sheets back and made a space for the child. "You two go back to bed," he said with resolution. "I'll go fill up her bottle and then check the house and outside."

"Don't be long," said Trish, her voice still twinged with fear.

He smiled at her as he closed the bedroom door behind him.

Standing in the glare of the refrigerator light, Gabe puzzled over the strange occurrence. She'd babbled a lot when she was new-born, stared at fixed points where there was none, but they'd dismissed it as being normal. His grandmother, though, had other theories. "She's talking to angels," she would say with a glint in her eye. "Your children both can." She was a kind woman who had run a nursery school when she was younger. It seemed that many of the fairy tales and superstitions had stayed with her all these years.

He stepped back across to his bedroom and opened the door. Shannon was still awake, although barely, and Trish was drifting as well.

He gave the bottle to the toddler, bent and kissed his wife goodnight, pulled on his dirty jeans and a shirt, and went out of the room, bat in hand, to see if there was really some kind of strangeness afoot. He glanced up at the clock in the kitchen. 2:30. It was too bad he had to work in the morning.

Crossing back to Shannon's room, the sounds of whispering they had heard played on his mind. Had it just been static on the old monitor? Had they really heard voices? He cautiously opened the door. The little night-light still burned and the room looked as it did when he left it: boxes and toys, but nothing else. No intruders to be found here.

He made his way through the maze of boxes and toys to the bathroom and opened the door. The old hinges squeaked, making his heart quicken. So much for surprise, he thought. After a brief inspection of all the cupboards and cabinets, he was satisfied there was no one else in the room. He made sure the door to the adjoining room was locked and made his way back out of the room.

Gabe padded across the dining room and into the living room. He could see better in here, as there were no curtains on the windows and the dim light of the moon filtered in. At the far end of the room, by the front door, was the door to Lizzy's room. He crept across the bare boards, pausing to make sure the front door was locked, and put his hand on the knob of his oldest daughter's door. A chill went up his arm and made the hair on his neck prickle. He listened intently to the silence in the air. Was that a whisper he heard? Or perhaps footsteps? He opened the door and peered inside.

Lizzy lay sleeping in her bed, her blankets twisted about like rope as she kicked them off in her sleep. Gabe surveyed the room intently. Boxes and clothes, bits of jewelry and CDs were strewn about. He smiled. It was probably the cleanest her room would look from this point on. He put the bat beside the door and crossed over to her bed, where he quietly unwound the blankets and tucked them over his sleeping angel. No sign of disturbance here, he thought, as he looked around the room. The closet and bathroom doors were open and readily visible, betraying no hidden predators.

He went to exit, reaching for his bat, and felt his stomach knot and the hair on his arm stand on end. It was not there. Panic streaked through his body. Someone's here, he thought, but how? His head jerked first one direction then the other, searching for someone, something, his lost bat. At the foot of Lizzy's bed, he saw it leaning quietly against the post. He felt his skin begin to creep. I must have put it there, he thought. Taking the bat in hand, Gabe exited as quietly as he could manage and continued his rounds of the house.

As the door closed behind him, his thoughts were whirling. Had he put the bat by the door? Had he heard whispers? He caught movement out of the corner of his eye and leaped back, slamming into a stack of boxes, bat raised. His reflection in the window postured back at him. Gabe felt himself flush.

Stupid, he thought. Now you're jumping at your own reflection. Just calm down. He unlocked the front door and stepped out onto the wide porch. The night was cool and a haze hung in the air, giving everything a surreal feeling. He fished the crinkled pack of cigarettes out of his pocket. Smoking was forbidden in the house. His children didn't need the stench of burnt tobacco on them, and he wanted to keep the house smelling clean. He lit the cigarette and took a long drag. Just calm down, he thought again. You're making yourself paranoid.

He walked the length of the enormous porch, scanning the yard for any signs of a presence. Too many shrubs and bushes to tell, he decided, and walked slowly down the steep front stairs and into the yard. The grass was cool and moist on his bare feet as he walked the perimeter of the yard, pausing at every questioning shadow and poking every shrub with his bat. Outside the house he felt more at ease. He still felt as though he were being observed, but the watcher was farther away, less likely to make contact. He looked up at the old house.

"What are you doing with us?" he muttered.

As if in answer, he thought he saw a shadow move past the window in the living room. It could have been a trick of the light, or a figment of his sleep-deprived mind. Regardless, he dropped the butt, raced up the stairs and threw the door open, bat held high. Lizzy squeaked and spilled her milk.

"Daddy!"

Again, Gabe felt stupid. He'd almost bludgeoned his own child.

"Hi, honey," he said, slowly lowering the bat. "What're you doing up?"

"I was getting a glass of milk. What're you doing up, with a bat?"

"Nothing," he lied. He didn't want to upset her further by telling her there might be an intruder in the house and Daddy couldn't find him. "Night practice."

Lizzy fixed him with such a look of incredulity that he became self-conscious. "You are so weird sometimes," she muttered, heading off to her room.

"Hey," Gabe broke in. "No food or drinks in the rooms anymore, remember? It's time to break bad habits in the new house. You'll have to finish it in the kitchen."

Lizzy grunted and stooped her shoulders. This was an inconvenience to her and she was letting Gabe know in no uncertain terms how she felt about it. She turned abruptly and shuffled toward the kitchen with Gabe right behind her.

In the kitchen they sat on stools at the makeshift island in silence. Finally, Gabe spoke.

"So what woke you up?"

"I don't know," she replied. "I just did. I was asleep one minute, and the next I was wide awake. You?"

"Oh..." he began, not sure of how to ward off the question. "I just couldn't sleep. New house and all, y'know?"

"Yeah. I think that must be it with me too." She looked back to her milk.

Gabe looked long and hard at his daughter. She was to him, as all children are to their parents, the definition of beauty, with long golden hair and amethyst eyes. Her pudgy cheeks still showed her youth, but it was clear the beautiful woman she would grow up to be. Even with her hair standing on end and pointing in a thousand different directions, a condition she referred to as "bed-head," she was lovely.

She was nearly two years old when Gabe and Trish met, the product of another relationship that went bad. He hadn't wanted children before meeting her, and had never wanted to date a woman with children. Something about her had captured his heart. Her mother was a wonderful lady, thoughtful and understanding, but it was Lizzy who had clinched the deal. It was a happy coincidence that their features were similar, and even more astonishing that they had the same birthday, exactly twenty years apart. It had seemed to Gabe that this child was destined to be a part of his life, and he was thankful every day that she was in it.

Lizzy stood up and took her empty glass to the sink.

"Daddy," she asked. "When can Bishop come?"

Gabe sighed. The damned cat. "I'll pick him up tomorrow on the way home from work."

Her milk finished and a kiss goodnight later, Lizzy went back to bed, leaving Gabe alone. The more he thought about it, the more he was sure it had all been his imagination. In their half-wakened state, he and Trish had heard static and transformed it into whispers. He put the bat on the island, padded across the concrete floor to the back door and went outside. He crumpled up the now-empty cigarette packet and lit the last butt.

The night was still dark. Through the window he could see the clock in the kitchen. 4:33. It was hardly worth trying to go back to sleep, seeing as how he would have to get up again by six. He took a long drag. Imagination, that was all it was. He began to relax a little. There was no one in the house, save for his family, and everyone was safe.

His cigarette finished, he went back inside, careful to lock the door behind him, and made his way back to the bedroom. Trish was asleep with Shannon cuddled in her arms. He quietly closed the door, removed his shirt and jeans and slid gently into bed next to his wife and child. He had so convinced himself it was just his imagination playing tricks on him that he hadn't noticed his bat was no longer lying on the table where he had left it.

From high above, it watched them sleep, the mother, the father, and the baby. It wished these would stay, but knew they had to leave. They had to get out. The woman shines, though not as greatly as the baby. The father, though…how protective he is, plunging headlong into something he cannot possibly comprehend. He was fortunate it was not the other he tried to drive away with his club. Best to put that away, out of his reach lest he hurt someone, or someone hurts him.

It flitted like smoke through the house, unseen, unheard. The fourth, the oldest child, shines, though not so brightly. She is too angry, too at-odds with herself. Still, she seems to be unafraid of anything. The other can use her, can use them all. It will be the oldest child that it wants most. The children are in danger. It knows a most terrible rage and jealousy. The father it will try to kill.

Amid the rubble deep within the basement, something stirred. It began, as many things do, small, with a mote of dust catching a breeze and shifting into a circular pattern. An awakening from fitful sleep, caused by new energies.

CHAPTER 5

THE MORNING WAS WELL BEGUN. Gabe had tried not to wake Trish before leaving for work, but she heard his alarm clock go off and wanted to make him breakfast, so while he was in the shower, she carefully climbed out of bed so as not to wake Shannon, pulled on her terrycloth robe and slippers, and went to the kitchen.

Coffee was made, as she'd set the automatic pot the night before, so she poured herself a mug and got out a pan to cook eggs. It may have been a terribly outdated role, the wife cooking for the husband, but Trish genuinely enjoyed doing it. Besides, she knew that if she didn't make breakfast for him, he'd either eat something unhealthy from a vending machine or just not eat at all. Occasionally he'd chide her, reminding her she was his wife, not his servant, but it was one of the little pleasures she took in life.

The previous night's events played in her mind. She hadn't noticed when Gabe came to bed, but she knew he'd been up late. If he had found anything, he would have told her immediately. So what had she heard, she wondered. Could it have been static, a draft, or even just her imagination? She decided on the latter and set to work cooking for her husband: three eggs over hard, toast, and coffee. She was just scooping the eggs into a plate when she was startled by a voice from behind.

"I was trying to let you sleep," said Gabe. He was fully dressed, ready for the day with the exception of his still-wet hair. It was his custom to let it dry on the way to work.

"I know."

He crossed from the doorway over to her and kissed her cheek.

"Y'know, you're my wife..."

"'...not your servant,' I know," she said. "And I keep telling you, I like cooking for you. I love you."

He smiled sleepily. "I love you too, hon."

Gabe sat down at the island and rubbed his eyes.

"How late were you up?" asked Trish, bringing over his plate and coffee. She sat down across from him.

"Late enough," he said. "About four-thirty."

"Did you find anything?"

"Nope," he said between bites. "I think we both imagined it."

"Really?" she asked, sipping her coffee thoughtfully.

Gabe finished his breakfast, rinsed his plate, and kissed his wife goodbye as he shuffled out the door to go to work.

While the children were still sleeping, Trish decided to finish her coffee and take a shower. Moments of solitude were rare for her, as Shannon always seemed to want her mommy within sight and Lizzie, though more capable, always had some issue to discuss. She refilled her coffee mug and made her way quietly into the bathroom.

Of all the places in the house, this room seemed to make the least amount of sense. It was as long and wide as any bedroom, but poorly laid out. Immediately through the door was the toilet facing the first mirror and sink. Further in were two closets, both cavernous and unfinished, but useful at any rate. Beyond them the room widened. Trish shook her head at the hot tub and smiled in bemusement. Across from it was a shower stall and a second vanity sink.

She took a sip of her coffee and set the mug beside the sink, opened the shower's smoked glass door and turned on the water. One of the problems with old houses, she thought. It takes the water a little while to warm up. She untied her robe and hung it on the peg next to the shower door. She took another sip of coffee and brushed her teeth. As she bent to spit the last of toothpaste and water out of her mouth, she caught movement out of the corner of her eye, just there, in the mirror. Trish jerked her head up so quickly that she nearly fell backward into the shower.

There was no movement in the mirror, save for her own eyes twitching. She scanned the reflection of the entire bathroom, almost fearing to turn around lest some unseen goblin leap out at her. She slowly turned and searched the rest of the bathroom, but there were no monsters or bogymen.

She glanced toward the shower. Steam was beginning to rise from behind the smoked glass door. That must be what I saw, she thought. Steam out of the corner of my eye. She glanced around, still unsure, as she pulled the oversized t-shirt that she wore as a nightgown over her head. Was it new house jitters that made her feel like she was being watched, made her hear voices in static, made her jump at wisps of steam? She took a deep breath, exhaling her nervous feelings.

In the mirror, as she had done a thousand times, she looked at her body and frowned. Two children had made her tummy bulge more than she would like. Her breasts seemed to her to hang lower every day, an observation her husband did not agree with. He'd smile at her and tell her how beautiful she was, reminding her he would always find her beautiful. She was still pretty, she decided, but not the taut thing she'd been eleven years ago.

She had traded her skin-tight blue jeans for the comfort of sweat pants and the joy of motherhood, a trade she considered more than fair. Being a wife and a mother meant everything to her. Her children were a gift from God, and her husband, although by no means a saint, was a good man with a good heart, and he'd pledged it all to her.

She stepped into the shower and closed the door, drinking in the warmth of the water as a plant soaks up sunshine. She washed her short blond hair vigorously, massaging her scalp with her fingertips. A good, long, hot shower was a sweet indulgence, she'd often said, and one not often afforded to the mother of two. As the water ran down her head, washing the bubbles from her hair and down her face, she heard the bathroom door open.

"Mommy's in the shower!" she called out, a little annoyed at the intrusion.

When there was no answer, she grumbled and washed the soapy water from her face and eyes. There, on the other side of the smoked glass she could make out a figure, small, about the size of a child.

"Shannon," she said, exasperated. "Go out of here. Mommy's taking a shower. I'll be out in a minute."

The figure made no reply. She could see well enough to notice that the child's back was to her.

"Shannon," she said again with more force. "Go out of here. Let mommy take a shower!"

Without a word, the figure turned. Trish's skin began to creep. Even through the smoked glass, she could see this figure was not her daughter. It was nothing so much about the general shape or hair color of the tiny figure that set it apart from a normal child. It was the way it moved, at one moment impossibly slow, at another spastically twitching with electric speed. Even through the smoked glass, Trish could make out its eyes, not in detail, but that they seemed to be pure white light.

Trish threw open the shower door. Where the apparition had stood there was nothing. Not even a dent in the thick shag of the bathmat gave evidence that anyone or thing had been standing on it. Trish turned off the shower and got out gingerly, her eyes still wide and searching for the presence. She grabbed her robe and hastily put it on, tying the belt around her waist. She was alone in the bathroom. There was no presence, no little girl. The bathroom door remained closed and locked. Had she fallen asleep in the shower, she wondered. Had she dreamed the figure behind the glass? She took a towel off the rack, wrapped it around her dripping head and exited the bathroom.

Shannon was sleeping soundly on Trish's bed, still clutching her bottle in one hand and the strange tattered doll in the other. Trish went out and made her way to Lizzy's room. She quietly opened the door, only about an inch, so she could see. There slept her oldest child, still softly snoring. It couldn't have been either of them, she thought. They're still asleep. And besides, the door was locked. How would they have gotten in?

She gingerly closed the door and quietly padded back to her room. That has to be it, she thought as she closed the door behind her. I must have fallen asleep and dreamed the whole thing. She made her way back into the bathroom and stopped cold in her tracks. There, in the freshly steamed mirror, a small finger had drawn a heart.

THE OFFICE TELEPHONE WAS RINGING AGAIN. Gabe reached without looking and picked up the receiver.

"Gabriel Rosewood," he said.

"There's something in the house," came the frightened voice on the other end of the line.

"Calm down, honey," he said, instantly focused on his wife. "What happened?"

"I got in the shower," she began, her voice trembling, "and looked up and there was someone there! I thought it was Shannon, but she was asleep, and when I opened the door it was gone." She began crying. "And it drew hearts on the mirror, and..." she sobbed. "Please come home."

"Where are you now?" He was already out of his chair and grabbing for his briefcase.

"I'm in the kitchen," she sniffed.

"Are the kids with you?"

"Yes."

"Good. Keep them there. I'll be home in five minutes."

"Thank you," she cried softly.

"I love you, honey." He hung up the phone. He wasn't sure what had happened, only that his wife was frightened to tears. What had she said? Someone was in the bathroom with her? Someone or something? And it had drawn on the mirror? He had no time to puzzle it out. He ran out of his office, taking only enough time to lock his door. As he passed his boss's office, he called out to the secretary.

"I'm leaving. Trouble at home."

Without waiting for a reply, he raced down the stairs and out of the building to his car. He pulled into the driveway at the old house to find Trish and the kids on the terra-cotta patio in the back. The children, still dressed in their pajamas, were playing in the backyard. Trish, wearing only her terrycloth bathrobe, was sitting at the edge of one of the patio chairs smoking a cigarette. She looked terrified.

"What happened?" he asked, not even fully out of the car yet. "What're you doing outside?"

The children ran to their daddy, clutching at his legs and waist.

"Daddy!" said Lizzy. "It was so cool!"

"It most certainly was not!" shouted Trish, wrapping her arms around Gabe and hugging him fiercely. "We were waiting in the kitchen like you said, and then there were all these noises. Banging and stomping, and the house was shaking..." Her voice trailed off. "It was like there was someone in the house throwing a tantrum."

Gabe looked the house up and down. He'd never seen his wife in this state, and he didn't like it. His children seemed unfazed by the event. Lizzy beamed with excitement and Shannon sat quietly playing with the odd little doll.

"I'll go have a look," he said with finality.

Trish held him tighter. "No," she nearly shouted. "I don't want you to go back in there. I don't want any of us going back in there."

He pried his wife loose. "Honey," he said looking sternly into her eyes, "I have to. If there's someone in there, I'll find him. If there's not, I'll find the cause of the noise. Either way, I have to go in there."

"Can I go with you, Daddy?" asked Lizzy.

He smiled. "Not this time, sweetie. Wait here with Mommy and help her with your sister." She stamped her foot and stomped off to sit dejectedly by her sister.

"Please don't go in there," said Trish with urgency.

He held her face in his hands. "Don't worry. Nothing's going to happen to me." He kissed her. "Besides, someone's got to go in there and get you some clothes."

Trish was not amused. Gabe smiled at her reassuringly, though inside he was a bundle of raw nerves. What was happening to his family, he wondered. He crossed the patio quickly, determined not to betray the feeling of nervousness inside. If there was something in the house, he would find it, he thought, but then what? He reached for the doorknob, as if he expected it to bite him. He took a deep breath and, eyes wide, cautiously opened the door and peered inside.

The house was quiet. There were no noises, save that of the air conditioner, no flying furniture, no evidence anything was out of the ordinary. Whatever the tantrum was, it had stopped. Trish had a tendency to let her mind blow things out of proportion, he knew, but he had never seen her in such a raw panic before. Something had happened here, but what it was he could not be sure.

He made a quick check of the house, taking special care to check the children's rooms before going into his own room. This was where the trouble started, he said to himself. If he was going to find anything, it would be here.

Nothing seemed out of the ordinary in the room. The bed covers were rumpled, the imprint of Shannon still on his pillow. Clothes from the night before peeked out of the hamper at the end of the bed. But there were no monsters, no presences, no fit-throwing beings of any kind he could see. Only wet footprints that went to the door, Trish's, he assumed, gave any hint that her story was true.

He went into the bathroom and looked for some sign of intrusion. He stood in front of the shower, facing the mirror, trying to discern what she had seen. There was nothing. He did see a shadow from a moving tree branch in the window, but nothing that even vaguely resembled the little girl described by his wife.

He knew she was telling the truth, or her own perception of it, but there was simply nothing there. Not even the sense of being watched that he normally had in the old section of the house was felt now. All he could feel was empty air.

He made his way out to the back door. Through the picture window, he could see his family standing, talking to a lady he'd never seen before. She turned and smiled at him as he opened the door.

"Morning!" she beamed. "Lots of excitement around here this morning, isn't there?"

"I guess so," he said, looking to Trish. She looked sheepish.

"Honey," she began. "This is Veronica. She lives next door."

"Hi," he said, shaking her hand.

Veronica was an older lady, perhaps in her late fifties, with dark hair peppered with gray. From the darkened wrinkles around her eyes, Gabe could tell she smiled often, so he felt her happy greeting was normal behavior for her.

"Veronica was just telling me what all that shaking in the house was about." It was obvious that the more she thought about it, the more embarrassed she became.

"Well, not too many people realize that this whole city is built on a fault line," she explained cheerily.

"Fault line?" echoed Gabe.

"Oh yeah," she said. "We get minor tremors like the one this morning every so often. I've lived here so long, I hardly even feel them anymore."

"I see," he said, looking at Trish with bemusement on his face. She looked at her feet.

"Yeah," continued Veronica. "I can always tell when one of those things is about to get nasty because all the old pipes in my house," she pointed to the neglected house on the corner, "rattle like they're going to come apart."

"You don't say," he said with a chuckle. He put his arm around his wife. "As long as everyone's alright."

"Well, it was nice to meet you," said Veronica. "Sorry it had to be like this. Maybe some time you can come over and have coffee?"

"That would be nice," said Trish quietly.

Veronica waved as she walked back to her house, leaving Gabe and Trish standing on the patio. The children were playing in the little play house.

"I'm so sorry," said Trish without looking up, clearly mortified.

Gabe pulled her to a close embrace. "It's alright," he said. "I was looking for a reason to get out of the office anyway."

"I feel so stupid."

"Why? I imagine it was pretty terrifying."

"Yeah, well..."

"Now, what was this thing you saw in the bathroom?" he asked.

Trish stiffened again. "I don't know. I swear I saw something while I was in the shower."

"Come inside," he said. "Get dressed and show me what you saw." He looked up to where the children were still playing. "Lizzy," he called. "Bring your sister inside. It's all clear now."

"Okay," she called back.

"Since you two are up," he said while holding the door for them, "you may as well get dressed. Lots to do today."

While Trish was putting her clothes on, Gabe took Shannon to her room, changed her diaper, which was heavy from the night's sleep, and dressed her in little orange shorts and a matching flowered shirt, little fold-down socks, and her favorite Winnie-the-Pooh canvas sneakers. Once dressed, he left her room to rejoin his wife.

"Brush your hair!" he called out across the house as he crossed the dining room. It was a sore spot with Lizzy because her hair was so thick and wavy that brushing it hurt. She would have liked to not brush it at all.

Trish was sitting on the bed pulling on her socks when he came in. He went past her into the bathroom, straight to the back where the shower stood.

"I was in the shower," he heard her voice behind him, "and I saw... something."

He opened the shower door and climbed inside.

"You were facing this way?" he asked, turning toward the mirror and sink.

"Yes."

Gabe closed the door. He could see her through the smoked glass, but with no clarity. It would be easy, he thought, to mistake a shadow for someone standing there.

"And it moved," she continued. "Not like a normal movement, but all jerky, then slow."

He opened the door.

"Jerky?" he asked. "Kind of like the leaves on a tree?"

She looked at him, dumbfounded.

He climbed out of the shower stall and walked over to the hot tub, climbing up on its rim to reach the small windows in the corner above it.

"I think what you saw, " he said, peering out the window, "was the shadow of one of these trees. Maybe a squirrel."

"I don't know," she said, her confidence already shaken by the tremor. What if she had imagined the whole thing? "I suppose it could have been." Her voice trailed off. "What about the heart in the mirror?" she asked, her voice sounding desperate to prove there was at least some shred of her story that could not be explained away as her own silly imagination.

"Honey," Gabe smiled. "If you draw something on the mirror with your finger when it's dry, steam will make it appear. I used to do that to my brother when we were kids. Used to freak him out, too."

She looked around the room feeling silly and dejected.

"I'm so sorry," she repeated.

"Stop apologizing," he said, drawing her close. "That's one of the good things about working for the University. I can leave whenever I want."

"Daddy," came Lizzy's voice from behind them. "Are you still going to get Bishop today."

"Yes," he said in exaggerated exasperation. "I'll pick him up from the vet today. Happy?"

"Thank you!" she beamed as she spun on her heels and skipped out of the room.

"That child is more persistent than a pit-bull," he said, smiling.

"I know," said his wife.

With her assurance she was fine and would not allow her imagination to get the better of her again, Trish convinced her husband to go back to work. It was just silly for him to stay, now that her fears had been quelled. She watched him back out of the gravel driveway and head off toward the college. There were still questions in her mind, ones that could not be answered by shadows or fault lines, but she was certain they would be answered logically in time.

CHAPTER 6

Only the most cursory of explanations had been required for his hasty departure that morning, and Gabe spent the rest of the day dealing with the usual problems, most of them from human error, that his job dictated. By the time he left he felt mentally drained. He'd almost forgotten his promise to Lizzy, but remembered when he passed the vet's office on his way home. He'd had to circle the block to get back to the office, but he'd kept his promise, and now he was driving home with Bishop sitting silently in his carrier in the seat beside him.

Hard to believe, he thought, that, when I got him, this cat would fit in my shirt pocket. He glanced over at the giant crate that was his traveling companion now. Seventeen pounds later, he just wasn't as cute anymore.

Bishop had been a gift to Lizzy for her eighth birthday. They'd just bought a house and she had complained that she wanted a pet. Gabe, being the soft touch he was, especially toward his daughter, went out and found a family giving away free kittens. The little black and white ball of fluff had been the only one that wasn't immediately afraid of him. He had come home that day to find Trish at home instead of at work.

"I have a surprise for Lizzy," he said, lifting the kitten for his wife to see.

"I have a surprise for you," said Trish, dropping the results of her pregnancy test in his hand.

Gabe could only blink as he said, "Your surprise is better than mine."

Lizzy was thrilled, of course, with the news of Shannon's impending arrival, but it was the new kitten that she was mostly interested in. At her age, she didn't quite comprehend how greatly her life would change with the addition of another child. Bishop had spent the night curled up in the corner of Lizzy's bed next to her face.

"Try not to make too much of a mess," Gabe muttered at the cat as they pulled into the driveway behind the house. He parked and got out, walking around to the passenger's side to get the crate, then carried it down the steps across the patio to the back door. "You're going on a diet," he muttered.

As he reached for the back door, Bishop made a peculiar sound deep in his throat. Gabe had heard it before, when the cat was threatened by another cat or when it was angry.

"What's with you?" he asked, peering at the cat through the bars of the carrier. Bishop's ears were laid back, his yellow eyes so wide they looked only black. As he reached again for the door Bishop hissed.

Ignoring the cat, Gabe stepped through the door.

"Lizzy!" he called. "There's a worthless piece of fluff waiting for you!" He really did like the cat, but he liked aggravating his daughter more. He set the cage on the floor and opened it. When Bishop didn't come out, Gabe looked at him quizzically.

"Bishop!" cried Lizzy as she came bounding into the room. "C'mere little kitty."

"Little?" asked Gabe teasingly. "That thing weighs more than your sister."

Lizzy was crouching in front of the carrier.

"Why won't he come out?" she asked.

"I don't know. New house maybe?"

"I know what might help," said Trish. "I was making tuna sandwiches for dinner anyway. Try to give him some."

Lizzy took a chunk of meat between her fingers and crouched again in front of the cage. Bishop slowly poked his fluffy head out the door.

He looked around suspiciously, sniffing the air, then slowly slunk to where the little girl was sitting, greedily eating the tuna morsels. Lizzy scooped him up around his middle and carried him off.

"Come see my room!" she bubbled as she left her parents alone in the kitchen.

"Well that was weird," said Trish, turning back to the pickles she was chopping.

"Yeah. He hissed at the door too," replied Gabe thoughtfully.

After a few moments, Gabe went to their room to follow his daily ritual of emptying the change from his pockets, removing his jewelry and generally getting comfortable. He noticed Trish had somehow managed to get all of the boxes unpacked and their contents put away. He smiled.

Being unemployed weighed heavily on her conscience, but she really enjoyed doing the day-to-day activities of being a full-time mother and wife. He wished he made enough money to let her stay at home. He changed into a pair of shorts, making sure that his pants hit the hamper, and went into the bathroom. Sure enough, Trish had put everything in its place here too.

He pulled his shoes back on. He had lots of work to do in this house, and if he was going to figure out what all there was, he'd better get down to it. He pulled a spiral-bound notebook off his desk, picked up a pen, and made his way to the front of the house. As he passed through the dining room, he looked in on Shannon, napping peacefully in her bed, the strange little doll nestled in her arms. He crossed the living room, listened for a moment to Lizzy begging the cat to come out from under the bed, and went outside.

The paint on the front porch had, at one time, been red, but bright sun had faded its color to a dark pink. Water had caused the boards to bow, as they had never been sealed, and the paint chipped off in places. He lit a cigarette and paced along the front porch, tapping his feet where the boards felt weak. As he came to the end, he saw a rather large rotted space on the planks. He crouched down to get a better look. He frowned as he opened his notebook and scribbled. *Replace front porch boards*. That would have to be the first thing, for safety's sake.

He stood up and examined the black rails that ran the length of the porch and down the steep stairs. *Sand and repaint rails.* He wondered if Toby had known how much work this place was going to be. He leaned against one of the great white pillars and was shocked when it shifted under his weight. Upon closer inspection, he discovered the roof was warped in such a way that several of the pillars were only held up by balance and slight pressure. Most of them were cracked and in need of paint. He shook his head. *Pull pillars, paint, fix roof.* He was puzzling out how to accomplish this feat when the door flew open abruptly.

"Dinner!" cried Trish, unaware of how close he actually was.

Her shout startled him, causing Gabe to back up a few steps. He was unaware of where he was standing, only of the look of horror on his wife's face and the sound of splintering wood as he felt his leg torn at by edge of the jagged hole. He cried out in pain as his right leg sank into the boards and the rest of his body fell hard on the porch.

"Oh Jesus!" she cried, leaping from the door to her husband. She grabbed his outstretched hand with both of hers and began to pull. Lizzy, hearing the commotion, ran out the door.

"Daddy!" she screamed, as she grabbed his other hand with hers and pulled with all her might.

"I'm alright," he lied through gritted teeth. He could feel splinters in his leg and hot crimson running down his calf. He'd be lucky if he didn't need stitches. "Find my notebook," he barked to Lizzy, trying to give her some task that would make her feel important, but also take her out of harms way. She released his arm and ran down the stairs to find it sprawled open like a large paper moth on the front lawn.

Gabe planted his free hand beside him on a section of plank he hoped was not rotted and pushed himself up, wincing in pain as he felt shards of wood tearing at the flesh of his leg. Combined with his wife pulling, he was able to turn himself to sitting on the sturdy portion of the porch. He gingerly lifted his leg from the toothy hole to survey the damage. Trish hissed at the deep scratches that marked his shin and ankle.

"That's going to leave a mark," he joked grimly. He looked around to find Lizzy, notebook clutched in her arms as if it were the most important document in human history. He took the notebook and, retrieving the pen from behind his ear, scratched through a previous entry and added *Fix the goddamned porch!!!* then handed the notebook back to his daughter. "Go put that on the kitchen table, please," he said, sending her inside at a trot.

Trish helped him to his feet and, with his arm around her neck, they clumsily hobbled into the house.

Below the gaping maw of the hole in the porch was the unfinished basement. Drops of crimson had fallen into the dirt floor and had been soaked up, as if greedily drunk by a creature dying of thirst. Now the dust began to swirl, though there was no wind. New energy, new life essence, gave rise to this whirling vortex. Its matter became dark and tendrils of inky ribbon snaked through the air and latched onto the timbers that were the foundation of the house. As they found purchase, they began to sink in, filling the cracks and veins, cancerous as they climbed and permeated the soul of the house.

"We should take you to the hospital," said Trish, crossing the kitchen with a wet washcloth. "That looks pretty nasty."

Gabe waved her off. "No need," he said. "It looks worse than it is." He cleaned the blood from his shin and surveyed the damage. "I'll live."

"Are you okay, Daddy?" asked Lizzy, her eyes wide with horror at the site of the deep grooves in her father's leg.

He smiled reassuringly. "I'm fine, sweetheart. Nothing that a little neosporin and gauze can't fix."

He dabbed the antibacterial cream at the wounds, hissing at its sting, and wrapped his leg loosely in gauze. Then, tearing the tape with his teeth, he fixed it into place and surveyed his handiwork.

"Now," he said finally, as he put away the first-aid kit, "you said something about dinner?"

Trish smiled sheepishly. "I'm sorry I startled you," she said, carrying plates with tuna sandwiches on them to the table.

"It's okay," he said. "It's my own damned fault for being so jumpy."

They ate their dinner in silence, each preoccupied with their own thoughts. Finally, after several minutes, Gabe looked around.

"Where's Shannon?" he asked Trish.

"She's still asl..." She didn't get to finish her sentence, because, as if in answer, the sleepy-eyed toddler came into view, her cheeks flushed and stained with tears.

"What's wrong?" asked Trish in her best concerned-mommy voice.

Shannon held her arms out and whimpered.

"Did you have bad dreams?" she asked, picking her up. Shannon shook her head.

"No? Then what is it, honey?"

She pointed to her room. "Bad."

Trish glanced at Gabe. "Bad?" she repeated, a look of worry across her face. "What bad?"

Shannon buried her face in her mother's neck and let out a deep sob.

Gabe got up from his chair and limped to the baby's room. As he opened the door, he wondered what horror awakened her. He clicked on the overhead light and looked around the room. Trish had managed to unpack the boxes that had stood piled high, the toys neatly put away in the giant purple bucket Shannon used as a toy chest. The room looked oddly bare, but there were no signs of "bad" that he could see.

"What is it, Daddy?" Lizzy asked as she poked her head beneath his arm from behind him.

"I don't know," he replied without looking at her. He was still searching for some sign of anything that would frighten his daughter.

"Ewww..." said Lizzy.

Gabe followed her expression to Shannon's little bed. There, on the blankets, was a pool of something black and sticky, a viscous fluid like tar. He limped slowly to the bed, Lizzy still attached to his belt loops. He dabbed at the pool with his finger, swirling the substance between his index finger and thumb. Wherever it touched it seemed to adhere.

"What the hell?" he muttered as he raised his blackened finger to his nose to see if the substance had any discernable odor. It's smell was pungent and sooty.

"It smells like burned motor oil," he said aloud.

He looked around the room, the ceiling and walls, for a possible source. Finding none, he began to look around the base of the bed, searching for some container that Shannon had gotten into without her mother's knowing. At the foot of the bed, beneath the leg closest to the inside wall, there was a smaller puddle. It looked to him like the fluid was seeping up through the basement, but that did not explain how it got on her bed.

"Go get your mother," he commanded, sending Lizzy for the next room at a trot. He set to work removing the soiled sheets from the bed.

"Honey," he said as his wife entered, Shannon still in her arms and Lizzy behind her. "Do you know what this is?" he asked, holding his thumb and forefinger to her for inspection.

She looked perplexed at the black slime. She smelled his fingers and made a sickened face.

"I have no idea," she said. "It smells..."

"Burnt," he said.

"Where's it coming from?"

"I don't know," he said, again looking around the room. "Here's a spot," indicating the floor beneath the leg of the bed, "where it's seeping up from the basement, but I can't find how it got on the bed." He pulled the sheets off. "What do you want me to do with these?" he asked. "Wash or toss?"

"Toss 'em," she said firmly. "I'm not putting that crap in my washing machine."

As Trish took the children to the kitchen to finish their meal, Gabe bundled the blankets together and wiped up the sludge on the floor. Having done that, he carried the bundle out through the kitchen to the outdoor garbage bin and went back inside. He was just about to sit down to finish his sandwich when he noticed the black substance was still on his hand. He went to the sink to wash it off.

The water was hot and scalded his skin, but still the stain remained. He tried scrubbing with a pot scrubber, but the stubborn blot would not come off. Finally, with a heavy sigh of frustration, he went to the garage. Moments later, he returned, smiling and smelling of gasoline.

"What did you do?" asked Trish, holding her nose.

"It wouldn't come off, so I poured gas on it," he replied.

"Did it work?" she asked.

"Yup." He went back to the sink and washed his hands again in warm water and soap, then went back to his waiting sandwich, the bread of which was now soggy.

Throughout the rest of the meal, they were entertained by Lizzy's theories about where the strange black ooze had come from and by Shannon's joyful giggling and kicking in her highchair. Once dinner was finished, Lizzy went to her room to play with her computer while Gabe sat in his ancient leather easy chair, watching television, with his leg propped up. Trish took the baby to the bathroom that adjoined her bedroom for her bath.

CHAPTER 7

LIZZY SAT AT HER DESK, the room dark except for the glow of her computer screen. She'd just managed to get it put together today, a priority for her, and was determined to make up for time lost while it was still packed. Her computer wasn't the fanciest model or the newest. In fact, it was pieced together from spare parts, other computers and components, built for her by her Uncle Toby. He thought it was important that she have one, and since neither he nor Lizzy's parents could afford to buy one, he set to work creating one that would suit her needs.

It was plenty fast and had a DVD-ROM drive so she could watch a movie or play games. Its outer shell was painted by Aunt Sarah with flowers of garish colors. All things considered, it suited Lizzy quite well. More importantly, it was hers and hers alone. These past two years she'd had to slide into the role of big sister without much choice in the matter, and had seen some of her old cherished toys reduced to pieces by her little sister's hands. But this... this was hers, and the baby could not touch it.

She loved her little sister, to be sure. She glowed with joy at carrying her around wherever they were and enjoyed playing with her in the sand box or in the little play house in the back yard. She sat in the floor while

Shannon jumped on her, all the while squealing in delight. Being a big sister was great fun to her. Most of the time.

At other times, she just wanted to be left alone. Not only by Shannon, but by her mother and father too. These were times when she wanted to be the baby again, when she didn't have to share, and Mommy and Daddy only had eyes for her. These were the times she would lose herself in her computer or in a book, usually dealing with the occult or fantasy worlds, or some other past time where Shannon would not pull at her hair and tear at her clothes. She loved her little sister, but sometimes found solitude more favorable.

She sat deftly tapping and moving the mouse, creating works of art in the paint program that was her favorite. She could hear the activities of house from her room; the splashing and giggling of her sister in the bath, the mock-scolding her mother gave at getting splashed, the noise from the television as her father sat, probably watching some wrestling program. She looked back to her bed where Bishop lay yawning lazily.

"Looks like they've forgotten about me," she said dejectedly. "Again."

She slid off her chair and plopped down on her bed, taking her cat in her arms. "You still love me," she said to green eyes set in fluffy white fur. Of course she knew her parents still loved her. She knew they had not really forgotten, but they regarded her as self-sufficient and not as needy as the baby. While she enjoyed being treated as an older person, she still craved the attention.

Bishop jerked his head toward the computer and hissed.

"What's wrong," Lizzy said, feeling the cat's muscles tense.

Bishop struggled to get free, digging his rear claws into Lizzy's arm, his eyes never leaving the part of the room where the computer lay. In pain, she dropped the cat who scrambled under the bed where it sat making an angry gurgling noise in the back of its throat. Lizzy's arm was bleeding, though not badly. She climbed off the bed in pursuit of her pet. As she peered under her bed, she could see only the reflection of light in his eyes. That, combined with the eerie noise issuing from him, was enough to make her flesh creep.

"Bishop... Kitty... You're scaring me."

She felt the hair on her arms prickle as the temperature dropped sharply. She slowly stood, her breath hanging in the air before her in misty puffs, and turned toward her computer. On the screen, her picture had changed. It was the picture she had drawn, but the colors were wrong, different somehow.

The house no longer seemed a happy little cottage, but an old rotting thing with angry eyes for windows and a howling mouth for a door. Where she had drawn bushes and trees were now black lines engulfed in shades of red and orange. In the eyes of the little house she could see faces, four of them, pressed against the glass, trapped inside. The image of Bishop hung from one of the burning trees.

She stepped backward, unaware that she was even moving. The cold seemed to press on her from all sides, crushing the breath from her body. Amid the din of her heart beating, she heard faint buzzing, a noise almost beneath perception, until it formed words.

"Lizzy..." It sounded like the wings of a thousand flies, buzzing in her mind. "Play with me."

She fell backward over the footboard of her bed, crashing into her mattress.

"Daddy!" she screamed.

As if broken by the sound of her voice, the cold spell abruptly vanished, returning the room to a comfortable climate. She looked around frantically as the tinkling buzz ceased as well. She heard limping footsteps cross the bare boards of the living room.

"Lizzy?" her father roared. "Honey? Are you alright?"

The door flew open revealing Gabe standing with a crazed look of panic and concern on his face. She leapt from the bed and into his arms sobbing as Bishop darted out the door between his feet.

"Oh Daddy," she said, trembling uncontrollably. "I was so scared."

"What?" he asked, looking around frantically. "What is it?"

"My computer," she said between sobs.

Gabe hobbled into the room toward the computer.

"What the hell..." he said frowning at the screen. He looked accusingly to Lizzy.

"That's not the picture I drew!" she pleaded.

"Then who drew it?" He sounded unconvinced.

"I don't know," she wailed through tears. "I drew a house with my kitty, and then Bishop freaked out, and the room got cold, and I looked and my picture looked like this." Gabe could see she truly had no idea where the gruesome scene on her computer had come from, and that she was growing more hysterical by the moment. With a click of the mouse he turned the computer off.

"It's okay, honey," he said holding her in his arms. "It's gone now."

"I didn't draw that," she continued sobbing, her eyes wide and staring at the now blank screen. "And it was so cold..."

He hugged her tight. "There's probably a draft in the house."

She pushed herself upright. "The voice," she said, as though just remembering.

"What voice?"

"There was a voice," she said intently. "It whispered my name."

"What the hell is going on in here?" Trish was standing in the doorway with Shannon wrapped in a towel in her arms.

"Something scared her," said Gabe, hugging his daughter close.

"Well it's no wonder," said Trish dismissively. "She's sitting in here alone in the dark in this creepy old house. I'd get the willies too."

"The willies?" Lizzy looked up to her daddy, who smiled at her and nodded.

"Pumpkin," he said. "The picture on your computer was probably caused by a virus or a glitch or something like that. That, along with the dark, and Bishop acting like a lunatic, I'd probably be hearing things too. We'll call Uncle Toby to see what's wrong with your computer." He glanced at his watch. "But not tonight. It's time for you to take a shower and get ready for bed."

All imagination, she thought, as her parents left her room. Had she imagined the cold? It didn't seem likely, but her parents were level headed and could always find explanations for anything. Still, something just didn't seem right. Try as she might to dismiss her panic as imagination, she still had a nagging doubt in the back of her mind, a pea under her mattress. She took a quick shower that night, a departure from her usual practice of bathing which usually took more than an hour. When she was finished, she dressed for bed and brushed her hair, made her hasty good-nights to her parents, and climbed into bed, her feet pulled up tight under her and the blankets over her head.

Sleep did not come easily, as the image of the burning house played in her mind and seemed to come to life in her imagination. She lay for a time singing softly to herself, a practice she'd learned from her Grandmother. It took her several choruses, before she finally drifted off to sleep.

CHAPTER 8

THE SCORCHING FLAMES SNATCHED at the tattered curtains in the house, climbing the walls in a blistering race. The air was thick and heavy with smoke as the inferno roared like an angry beast. The timbers of the kitchen ceiling fell, black and charred, as flames leaped into the next room and split, going either direction to do as much damage as possible.

As she ran through the blaze, Trish could hear screaming, although she could not tell from where or whom. She could see nothing through the smoke but only the dimmest of shapes. As the fire licked at her bare feet and cotton nightgown, she could only think in her terror to run, to get out.

A falling timber halted her as the fire seemed to grow and come alive around her, it's excruciating heat baring down on her with a weight that did not seem possible to endure. She could feel her clothing being charred away from her back. The din of the blaze filled her head, and still the scream cut through to fill her with sorrow.

"Where are you?!" she screamed.

The piercing shriek had no words, only the sound a child makes when it is in mortal terror. Trish reeled wildly as she searched for its source. She could feel the skin of her feet and back begin to peel.

"It's hopeless," she thought. "Hopeless." She felt the pain of her hair burning down to her scalp. She closed her eyes in acceptance. "We're going to die," she thought, surprised at how serene the words made her feel, at peace. She opened her eyes to see the wall of flame on all sides of her. Not even the house was visible anymore. There was no ceiling. Only flame and darkness. She smiled. "We're going to die, my baby and me," she thought again.

At once, the flames took shape and a face full of rage and hatred emerged from the fire. It loomed large in front of her, bellowing in defiance, but still she smiled. Columns of flame shot out like vines from the face and wrapped her arms in agony. She cried out as they shook her hard, as though trying to tear her body apart.

She screamed.

Gabe was holding her firmly by the arms and shaking her vigorously. Trish sat up, clawing at the air and her husband's face.

"Let us die!" she screamed, her eyes wide and unseeing. "Let us die!"

"Trisha!" Gabe shouted.

The force of her own name made her stop. She whirled about, but there was no fire, no demonic face of flames. She focused on Gabe. His face was bleeding with several shallow marks that ran down his cheek.

"Trisha," he said again. "You're dreaming. It's a dream."

"Gabe," she said, her eyes still reeling around the room. "My God..."

"It's okay," he said, his voice calm but intense. "It was all just a dream."

"What the hell...?"

"You tell me," he said, releasing her hands gingerly. "You were dreaming it."

"I don't know," she said, searching her mind for what she had seen. The images, however, would not come. Their memory was as much smoke in her mind, still there, but obscured somehow. She reached to touch her husband's face.

"Did I...?" she asked, indicating the bloody scratches down his cheek.

"Yes," he said recoiling.

"I'm so sorry."

"It's not your fault," he said, getting up toward the bathroom. "You were asleep. It's not like you meant to." He stood at the first sink and mirror, dabbing at the scratches with a damp washcloth. "What the hell were you dreaming about?"

She looked down at the blankets. "I can't remember," she said with frustration. "I just know it was horrible."

"It had to be, for you to do this." He came out of the bathroom, his wounds cleaned. "Whatever it was, if you remember it, write it down. I imagine it'd sell a million copies." He sat down on the bed next to her and pulled the blankets up over his legs. "Seriously, are you alright?"

"I don't know," she said, her voice shaky. "I think so."

"I've only got two hours before I have to get up for work. Can you sleep?"

"I don't think so."

"Would you like me to sit up with you?" The concern in his voice made her smile. "I don't mind."

"No," she said. "You need to be bright in the morning. Go on back to sleep."

She kissed him and he settled back down on his pillow. Within moments, he was snoring softly again, leaving Trish alone with her thoughts. Why couldn't she remember the dream, and why did it fill her with such dread?

She quietly got up, pulled on her terrycloth robe and slippers and went out of the bedroom, closing the door softly behind her. She took a deep breath, shaking the feeling of dread from her stomach, and walked quietly across the dining room to where Shannon lay sleeping. They had moved her bed away from the curious black spot, so she could see her plainly through the doorway, breathing deeply in slumber undisturbed.

She closed the door without a sound and walked across the living room to Lizzy's room and peeked inside. Lizzy had kicked the blankets off her in the night and now lay shivering in an upper corner of her bed. She crept into the room and placed the blankets back on her sleeping daughter, being careful not to wake her, and left the room. She went back across the living and dining rooms to the kitchen. Coffee would make her feel better, she decided. A cup of coffee and she'd be fine.

She set up the pot and measured out three scoops of coffee. Smiling at the aroma, she softly put the carafe into place, switched the pot on and waited until the first streams of liquid began to fall from the basket before moving to the cabinet to retrieve her favorite mug, the one that said "World's Greatest Mom" in gold paint. She sat at the island, the foggy memory of the dream floating wraithlike across her consciousness. She was lost in thought when Lizzy walked sleepily into the room rubbing her eyes.

"Hi mom," she said, sounding more annoyed than tired.

"What are you doing up?" Trish asked.

"Bad dreams."

Trish could feel the uneasy knot of dread return to her stomach. "About what?"

"Fire," said Lizzy, rubbing her eyes. "Lots of fire."

For a brief moment, Trish's dream flashed in her head. The smoke, the pain, the blazing face. "Fire?" she said again, the lump in her stomach growing.

"Yeah. I dreamed I was trapped in the house and it was burning." She took a glass from the cupboard and filled it with milk. "I was trapped in the house," she said, putting the milk away and moving to sit at the island beside her mother, "but I couldn't tell where. I was screaming for help."

"Then what happened?" asked Trish, her own nightmare beginning to take form in her head again.

"I saw you," she said looking up from her milk. "I saw you and you were on fire too, but you were smiling."

Trish felt cold needles prickling up her spine.

"But it wasn't you," she continued. "And it wasn't me. We were someone else." Lizzy sipped her milk. "What're you doing up?" she asked.

"I just couldn't sleep," she lied.

Lizzy looked up, her eyes widening. "You dreamed it too, didn't you?"

CHAPTER 9

GABE SAT AT HIS COMPUTER TYPING LINES OF CODE, his mind wandering to the scene he'd come upon that morning. After the horrific nightmare his wife had suffered, he'd managed to get back to a dreamless sleep. When his alarm did go off, he'd groggily gotten up and gone through his morning routine of showering and grooming, preparing for the day ahead. But when he emerged from his room, he was surprised to see not only Trish, but also his oldest daughter having what appeared to be an intense conversation. They went quiet when he'd come in the room, with only cheery greetings and little else to say. He left for work wondering what was going on, a feeling he suspected he would have more often as his girls grew older.

He looked back over the lines of code he'd written, cursing as he found several mistakes caused, no doubt, by his lack of concentration. As he moved the cursor back to his errors, he couldn't help but feel a little irritated. What was so damned important that they couldn't share it with him? It wasn't as if he was an uncaring sort. He'd helped through all kinds of problems before, so why couldn't they talk to him now?

His brooding was interrupted by a cheerful greeting at his office door. "Morning!" said the lanky older man leaning against the door frame.

"How's it going today?"

"Morning, Don," said Gabe without looking up.

Dr. Donald Thorndyke was a life-long academic, pursuing whatever strange course of study caught his interest. Over his life he'd managed to get doctorates in English literature and geography, and was currently studying parapsychology as a way to pass the time.

"Did you know this town was built on a fault line?" asked Gabe with intended drollness.

"Of course I did," Don laughed. "What happened? Did you get a little shake yesterday?"

Gabe nodded sharply.

"Geography, my boy. Geography." Don was in preaching mode now, something Gabe had become accustomed to, and in fact, regarded as one of his more endearing traits. It was always good to see a person passionate about what he did.

Don sat down in the rolling chair beside Gabe's desk, taking a long pull from his coffee mug.

"Yeah," Gabe began. "Trish and the kids were really shaken up by it."

"Any damage?"

"No," he said. Gabe looked up at his friend for the first time that morning. "But then," he said cautiously. "Then there were some other strange things that happened."

"Like what?"

"Well," he said. "Trish had this really severe nightmare." He turned to display his cheek. "She did this to me in her sleep."

"Might have been a by-product of the earthquake. My first one gave me nightmares too."

"That's what I thought," he continued. "But then, there's other things." His voice trailed off as he stared into his coffee cup. "I think this house may have been a bad idea."

"What other things?" Don asked, thoughtfully sipping his coffee. His interest was piqued.

"I don't know," he said, his voice trailing off. What should he tell him? They'd heard voices? About the black sludge? Maybe about Trish's mystery intruder in the shower? They all sounded ludicrous to him. He knew he could trust Don not to make judgments, but he didn't want to come off as sounding like an idiot. He decided to keep the strange occurrences to himself for now. "There's so much work to be done on it," he said instead, and raised the leg of his trousers to show the bandages. "This is what most of the font porch will do if you step on it."

"Ouch," said Don sympathetically. "Looks like you've got your work cut out for you. Anything else going on?" he asked pointedly.

"No," said Gabe, fighting the urge to blurt out how strange life in the house really was.

"Because, you know," continued Don, " you are living in the historic district of this town. Your house might be haunted."

"Yeah, right," said Gabe with a snuffling laugh. "You know I don't believe in ghosts."

"Famous last words," replied Don, smiling as he rose from the chair. "All the same, you might check out the history of your house with the hall of records, especially if you're going to be doing construction on it. The San Marcos Historical Society might actually help pay for restoration." He waved cheerily as he went out the door.

CHAPTER 10

On Don's advice, Gabe decided to take his lunch break to seek out the Historical Society. Even if there was no money to help with the restoration, he decided it would be good to find out the history of the house. Maybe there would be something of interest, especially to Lizzy. As he drove around the old town square, he found the office, marked with an old-fashioned shingle above the door.

If it had not been for the obviously new electric lights, Gabe would have felt that he'd stepped back in time when he entered the San Marcos Historical Society office. The musty smell in the air smacked of old newspapers and mildew.

It was amusing, he thought, that this place lived up to every stereotype he'd ever read about town preservation societies, from the antique furniture and oversized rugs on the floor to the elderly woman in a long dress who was now bustling toward him with a scowl on her face. The dark finish of the furniture stood out against the beige walls covered with old photographs of the town that was. Stepping into the room was almost like merging with one of the old yellowed pictures that showed people posing in their finery.

"Good morning," said the severe-looking woman. "I'm Mrs.

Habershine. How can the Historical Society help you?"

She was in her mid-seventies, Gabe guessed, with white hair done in a bun on the back of her head. She wore a gray taffeta dress, that, though not from any particular period, would have fit in well when the town began. Its high neck ended in black lace which just brushed the bottom of her slender jaw. The long sleeves ended similarly, making her wrinkled hands seem as if they were blooming from her arms. Her face was wrinkled and thin, with high cheek bones and considerable length.

"My name is Gabriel Rosewood," he said, extending his hand. "My family and I just bought a house in the historic district here and we're fixing it up..."

"The Historical Society has no more money to hand out," she cut him off crisply.

"I'm not here for money," he said after a brief pause. "I'm looking to find out the history of the house. Who built it, who lived there..." He smiled nervously, feeling that at any moment the old crone would leap upon him and tear him apart with her bony fingers. Her expression softened.

"Really..." she said with a raised eyebrow. She turned quickly, motioning over her shoulder for him to follow. "There are so many lovely houses here in San Marcos," she said as she walked. "Too many of them have been desecrated by fraternities, sororities, or even torn down by that goddamned college." She was clearly very bitter over the loss. "Too many people have no sense of their own heritage." She stopped by her desk and turned around sharply. "Where did you say you live?"

"On Blanco Street," he replied.

Mrs. Habershine stiffened. "Let me guess," she said. "316?"

"Yes," he said, taken aback. "How did you..."

"Because I know every house in the historic district of this town," she snapped. "And I know that 314 is kept in immaculate condition, and we couldn't be lucky enough for that... woman in 318 to have sold her house." She turned toward the large shelf behind her desk and began removing enormous volumes and binders. "Besides, you're not the first to come in here asking about the history of that house." She took the binder and book back out into the main office where a coffee table sat in front of a small couch. Dropping the binder on the table with a puff of dust, she gestured at him to sit. "Would you care for some coffee?" she asked with forced politeness.

"Yes, please," he said absently, his attention drawn to the book on the table as she hurried off. To call the book large would have greatly understated the case. Gabe had seen dictionaries that took up less space. He ran his finger across the gold leaf lettering on the worn leather cover that said "San Marcos: est. 1884." He opened the cover just as Mrs. Habershine returned and placed a mug of coffee in front of him.

"How do you take it?" she asked.

"Black," he replied, his eyes never leaving the pages.

She sat next to him, pulling the book from under his gaze and then flipping rapidly to the appropriate page.

"Your house," she said with authority, "was built in the 1930's by a man named Lennox. He lived there with his family, wife and two sons, until 1984. His sons had grown up and moved away, his wife had died, and he accidentally set the house on fire. He almost died in the blaze." She opened the binder and flipped through the old newspaper clippings within, stopping on the yellowed and faded image of the house, fire trucks in front of it with the headline "House Fire Claims No Lives."

"It was determined by his sons that he was no longer mentally competent to live alone, so they put him in a nursing home and sold it. It was sold to a family named McKenzie, though they never lived in it." She pointed to a place in her book where the name McKenzie was repeated several times. "They made their living, you see, buying houses on the cheap, making them livable, and selling them for a profit."

"Pretty shrewd," said Gabe quietly.

"They were vultures!" she half-shouted at him. "Making money off the misery of others, buying up family homes when someone fell on hard times..." She regained her composure. "It took them two years of work to get it back together after the fire, then in 1986 they put it on the market. It sat empty for sixteen years, nearly, until the Watermans bought it. They lived there for less than a year before they left as well."

"I wonder why no one ever bought it..." Gabe said, half to himself.

"I'm sure I don't know," she said sternly.

Gabe turned to face her. "Didn't anyone ever look at the house?"

"Of course they did," she replied incredulously. "The McKenzies even rented it out for a short while, but no one ever stayed."

"And when did the Waterman family move in?" he asked.

She looked in her book. "They took possession of the house in January of 2001. They moved out in May of that same year. Then, of course, as you'll see here, your family purchased it, although the name I have isn't Gabriel Rosewood. It's Thomas." She eyed him suspiciously.

"My father," he said. "My parents loaned me the money for the house. I'm paying the mortgage, but the loan is in their name."

"I see," she said derisively.

"Is there anything else you could tell me?"

"No." she said with finality.

After a pause, "Are you sure?"

"Absolutely," she said peering down her nose at him.

Another pause. "Well," he said, standing. "Thank you for the coffee and information." He wanted to say something, anything, to tell the old woman how he really felt, where she could put her snobbish attitude and holier-than-thou comments. Instead, he forced a smile and went back to his car, feeling as though his time was wasted. Professor Thorndyke would be in for an ear full when Gabe saw him again.

CHAPTER 11

LIZZY WAS OUTSIDE IN THE LITTLE PLAY HOUSE, cleaning. Trish smiled as she looked out the great bay window on her daughter, happily singing to herself as she swept. It amazed her that she couldn't get the child to clean her room, but given a project that seemed worthwhile to her, she would work with dogged determination. The shared dreams, the strange picture on her computer, even the bitter cold Lizzy had felt, were all but forgotten as she dusted tiny cabinets and brushed away cobwebs.

Trish, however, had not forgotten. Though she put up a brave front of having dismissed the phenomena, the memories of what was said and what happened bounced in and out of her conscious thoughts. Lizzy was stronger that she'd given her credit for.

She looked down to where Shannon sat in front of the television, watching cartoons and coloring, and smiled again. She was glad her youngest was too young to understand what was happening, or to have a real sense of the fear Trish was feeling. Since they'd moved her bed, there had been no more problems in her room.

She went back to organizing the kitchen as best she could. Some day, she thought as she opened another box, this kitchen will be finished, and I'll be very happy. She pulled a ceramic duck from the box and went to put it on the television, glancing down at her daughter as she did.

As she saw the orange marks on the paper, she could feel the now familiar tingle begin at the base of her neck. Shannon was staring at the television and absently moving the crayon in her hand. Though she was not paying attention to what she was drawing, words were clearly visible.

help fire burn

The words repeated over and over again across the paper while the toddler's hand continued to write them. As Trish crept closer, barely breathing, she could see that Shannon was oblivious to the marks on the page. Trish carefully, so as not to disturb her, slid the paper out from in front of her daughter and replaced it with another. Shannon's hand never quit moving, as if she never noticed her mother's presence.

As she watched, the child scribbled, much of it nonsense, but startlingly clear words cut through the garbled lines. *help* repeated, as did *fire*, but Trish's eyes welled with tears at the sight of one single word, followed by stillness of her child's hand.

mommy

"Baby?" she said, her voice trembling.

Shannon looked up smiling. "Hi mommy!" she beamed, then, noticing the tears in her mother's eyes, she threw her arms around Trish's neck and hugged her tight, nuzzling her face against her mother's neck. "Lub-ewe!" she said.

"Mommy loves you too," Trish said.

"What's going on?" asked Lizzy, entering the house.

"Look at this," she said as she stood, cradling Shannon in her arms. She held out the papers to Lizzy, who took them with a puzzled expression.

"What?" she asked. "It's just more refrigerator art," she said flippantly.

"Look closer," replied her mother intently.

Lizzy's eyes grew wide as she examined the pages, finally making out the words in the twisted lines of crayon.

"She did this?" Lizzy asked incredulously. Trish nodded. "When?"

"Just now."

"Man," said Lizzy, looking dejected. "I always miss the cool stuff!"

"Cool!?" her mother half-shouted. "This isn't cool! This is… terrifying!"

"I didn't mean…" began Lizzy as her mother grew more agitated.

"Is it cool that the house shakes? Or that we have nightmares of being roasted alive? Or that your sister is being possessed?" She was becoming hysterical. "What's so damned cool about it!?"

As if in answer, her tirade was stopped by the sounds of footsteps in the living room, fast approaching them. Trish held Shannon close to her and stepped in front of Lizzy, who peeked through the doorway from behind her mother's hips. The steps were hard and loud, thundering closer, though try as she might, Trish could see no source.

"Lizzy, get back," she whispered as the sounds grew louder and closer. "Take your sister." She handed Shannon over, her eyes never leaving the doorway. With the din of the thunderous banging in her ears, she stepped closer to the doorway, peering into the supposedly empty room, her fear tight inside her like knotted rope. Just when it seemed the falling steps would trample her underfoot, there was silence. As abruptly as it had begun, it stopped.

She stood in the doorway, listening intently for any hint of movement, any sound that might betray a presence, then turned to her children. "Well I wonder what that was," she said with forced calmness. No sooner had the words left her lips, than she was brought to her knees by an icy blast of wind from behind her, which felt as if it would rip the flesh from her spine. She could feel the breath sucked from her body by the shock of the blow. And then, another wind, this one so hot that she could feel her skin singe, came from in front of her, knocking her on her back. The door to her room slammed shut.

"Mommy!" cried Lizzy, running to her mother's side. "Are you okay?"

Unable to speak, she forced herself to turn over and lift her eyes to the ceiling as she heard what sounded like more footsteps, softer than the ones before, in the space above her room. She nodded.

"Yes," Trish said, gulping air. "Mommy's alright." She looked up at her daughters, both of their gazes fixed on the empty window above the door to her room.

They sat, transfixed for a moment, listening as the footsteps in the attic stopped, and the house was silent again. Lizzy was the first to speak.

"Mommy," she said timidly. "It's above your room."

CHAPTER 12

CRANKY OLD BITCH, THOUGHT GABE, sitting again at his desk, typing out lines of code. He was angry at having been treated so rudely by Mrs. Habershine, and that he'd used his lunch break to endure such mistreatment. Now he sat with coffee and a package of peanut-butter crackers he'd gotten from a vending machine, his stomach growling in protest. He didn't even notice when Dr. Thorndyke stood in his doorway.

"Bad day?"

Gabe didn't even look up. "I followed your suggestion... went to the historical society."

"And?"

"That crabby old bitch wouldn't tell me anything, except there is no money to be had to refurbish the house."

"Really?" Thorndyke smiled.

"Yeah," he said. Then, looking up, "And another thing, she is the most unfriendly, arrogant, stuck-up harpy I've ever laid eyes on. It's no wonder they're underfunded."

Don made a clucking noise with his tongue. "Well, that just won't do."

"It also seemed like she knew more than she was willing tell me, but damned if I could worm it out of her."

"You just have to know how to talk to these people," Don said, looking at his watch. "Do you have any more appointments for the rest of the day?"

"No."

"Good," he said. "Shut down your office and come with me." He stood and left the office. Gabe hastily shut down his computer, gathered his things and followed him out, locking the door behind him.

"What are we doing?" he called after him.

Don turned and smiled. "Going on a field trip," he said, disappearing into the secretary's office. Gabe waited for him outside. He'd already requested time off once this week, and didn't like to make a habit of such things.

When Don returned, he put his arm around Gabe's shoulder.

"Let's go," he said cheerily.

"What did you tell her?"

"The truth. That I'm doing some research and I require your assistance." His eyes twinkled. "I didn't say what I was researching, but it was essentially true."

They made their way to the parking garage where Don had parked his car. The black BMW seemed to suit Don's personality and status, but even more than that, it was just ostentatious enough to command the type of attention Don loved.

"Now tell me more about this person at the Historical Society," Don said as they went.

"Well," began Gabe. "She looks like she's about a thousand years old and dresses like Dracula's mother." Don sniggered. "She also has the warmth of an iceberg and the disposition of a wet housecat."

"We'll see if I can get any more information out of the old hag," Don said. "Like I said before, you just have to know how to talk to these people."

They pulled up in front of the Historical Society office. As Don turned the engine off, he gave Gabe a confident look and got out. Gabe was apprehensive, but followed his friend anyway. He really didn't want to see Mrs. Habershine again, but if Don could get her to tell the rest of the house history, he was willing to try.

When they entered the office, they could see a younger lady in more modern clothes sitting at the back of the office behind the computer and Mrs. Habershine, her back to the door, cleaning up the remnants of coffee and cookies, obviously from some new victim, from the table. Don walked briskly up behind her.

"Hello, you cranky old bitch," he said in a loud haughty voice.

Gabe's eyes grew wide as the recognition of what Don had said sunk in. He wanted to leave, to hide, to shrink to the size of a grain of rice and fall between the floorboards as she straightened and whirled on her heels to face Don.

"What do you want, you ignorant bastard?" she responded in kind.

Gabe was prepared to run from the store before they came to blows. Though Don was much bigger than she, he was sure that Mrs. Habershine would not go down without at least gouging his eyes out. Then he watched in stunned amazement as her sour face cracked into a smile and they hugged.

"Donald!" she said, her voice full of affection, as they hugged. "How are you? Where the hell have you been hiding yourself?"

"Hi, Doris," he smiled. "It's good to see you too."

"What brings you to this God-forsaken place," she said, releasing him, the smile never leaving her lips.

"My friend Gabe here," he said, gesturing to Gabe, who, though he had seen what had happened, could not comprehend it.

"Mr. Rosewood," she said, extending her bony hand. "How nice to see you again."

Gabe instinctively shook her hand, his brain still unable to wrap around what had just happened.

"Hi Kitty!" Don called out to the young woman behind the desk.

"Dr. Thorndyke," she said bristling. "My name is Katherine. Please try to remember that."

"Oops," he said. "Guess I forgot." He turned away from her and sniggered with a sideways glance to Mrs. Habershine. "Now, Doris," he said.

"What can you tell my friend and me about this house his family has just bought?"

She glanced quickly to Katherine. "I've told you everything I know," she said.

"Doris..." said Don with mock testiness.

"Please," said Gabe, finally able to find his voice. "It's really very important to me."

She leaned in close. "Just a moment," she said, then, sniffing the air, she asked "Do you smoke?"

Gabe looked up. "Um... yes," he said timidly. Don let out a snuffled laugh.

The old woman looked back at the younger woman behind the desk and turned a sly eye to him.

"Spare a cigarette for a kindly old lady," she smiled crookedly.

Gabe was charmed. He fished in his pocket for his pack and drew one out.

"Not in here," she said with urgency. "My daughter," she whispered, gesturing to Katherine. "She's the real bitch. If she even catches the faintest scent of smoke in the air, she'll have my head. Join me outside, won't you?" She turned purposefully toward the back of the office. "We keep all the large maps in the back," she said loudly, and led them all briskly past her stiff-lipped daughter and out the back door.

Outside, Gabe produced a cigarette for Doris and one for himself and lit them both. She took a long drag and with a satisfied smile she blew the smoke out her nose.

"Mmmmm," she said. "Thank you. I'm so terribly sorry about the way I acted this morning." She looked genuinely apologetic. "With all the students in this town, and all the fraternities trying to turn our beautiful old homes into party houses, it's difficult not to be defensive."

"Yeah, yeah," said Don, lighting his pipe. "That's what you always say. Truth is, you just like playing the grump."

"Oh, shut up," she said with mock irritation, "you old goat."

"So what about the house?" said Gabe, feeling a little awkward.

She took a long draw and glanced back at the door.

"You understand, of course, that this is strictly off the record," she said conspiratorially. "We at the society are not supposed to talk about the dirty secrets of this town. In fact, we're supposed to bury them."

Don leaned against the door, intensely interested in what the old woman had to say.

"What exactly did the real estate agent tell you about the house?" she asked, her eyes narrow, her voice as sharp as an icepick.

"She told me it was nearly seventy years old, that there'd been a fire..."

Doris huffed.

"...and that they'd had trouble selling it because of the price."

"That's not why," she said matter-of-factly. "Let me tell you a story. One hundred or so years ago, this town was founded by a small group of people who loved the rivers and hills this place had to offer. They called it San Marcos for the Spanish monks who had missions all through the Texas hill country. If you're ever interested, let me know. I'll show you where some of the lesser-known ruins are." She took another long drag of the cigarette, blowing smoke from her nose. "Even with a town so small, there had to be scandals."

Her gaze seemed to unfocus, as though the events were playing in her mind as she spoke. Her voice softened with the spinning of the tale, winding through the words as the smoke from her cigarette wound through the air.

"The family's name was Tinsley, Cyrus and Hester Tinsley. They came here with plans of a fresh life, striking it rich some way, and raising a family. They built a grand house for the time, with white pillars and a great porch, up on a hill where they could overlook much of the town. It took the better part of a year before the house was complete, but when it was, it was a thing to behold. They lived there for several years in quiet happiness, setting up a small general store and prospering as they had wanted to. Of course, at that time, the town was small enough that everyone knew everyone. There wasn't a soul that didn't know the Tinsleys, and when it was discovered that Hester was with child, the whole town rejoiced in their good fortune.

"When the child was born, there was no doctor in the town, so a midwife came to assist with the birth. It was said to be a long and painful labor, with poor Hester nearly losing her life." She paused, taking another long draw off the cigarette. "People said the pain caused Hester to change. They said she was never right in the head after that night.

"While Cyrus continued working at his store, Hester and their new baby, a little girl named Celia, faded from public life. Hester stopped receiving visitors and wanted only to stay at home with her child. When they did go out, she looked pale and drawn, sickly even. They never went out without their daughter. She was as beautiful as a porcelain doll. And wherever they went, Hester always kept a close, almost untrusting eye on her daughter.

"When the child was around eight years old, Cyrus perished in a riding accident. It was determined later that the horse he had been riding had managed to get a scorpion under his saddle blanket. It must have stung the horse, because it threw Cyrus into a deep precipice, presumably part of the fault line they now have opened up for tourists. It took them days to get his body out of there, but when they did, he was brought home for funeral arrangements.

"Of course the whole town came to the funeral. It was remarked by many that, as she sat in her heavy black gown holding the baby Celia in her arms, Hester didn't cry. She just sat staring blankly at the casket as they lowered it into the ground. Afterward, she hurried away, avoiding sympathetic words and looks, and retreated into the solitude of her home.

"Sightings of her around town became more sparse, and eventually stopped altogether. Then, one night about four months after the death of her husband, she set fire to her own house. No one really knows who reported it, but the fire brigade came, stymied by the steep hill the house sat on and the rocky terrain. By the time they made it to the house, it was far too late. There was no saving the house or its inhabitants. Some said they could see her in the upstairs dormer rocking peacefully in her chair, a serene smile on her lips as the fire gorged on the home. It burned down to the supporting timbers, killing Hester and poor little Celia."

Gabe stood with disbelief written on his face. "She killed her own daughter? Why?"

"Don't know," shrugged Doris. "Some say she wanted to be with her husband. Others say she was possessed. Some say she blamed her daughter for her husband's death. Who can say for sure?"

"So what about my house?" asked Gabe, the story still reeling in his mind.

"Your house," she said, forcefully blowing smoke out her nose. "Your house was rebuilt by the rest of the town on the supports of the original."

"I don't get it," he said, confused. "Why would they do that?"

She pointed with her cigarette. "The university, that's why. The state had already scouted areas to build their new teacher's college, and the town desperately wanted the prosperity that such a thing would promise. With the whole town's help, they rebuilt the house in less than a month, so when the committee came back through, they saw no signs there had ever been anything amiss. As far as they were concerned, this town was a little slice of paradise."

"What about Hester and Celia," broke in Donald, making Gabe jump. "Where were they buried?"

"They were buried in the family plot in the old cemetery on what is now called Ranch Road 12," she replied.

"It's horrible," said Gabe quietly.

"Yes," she said, crushing out her cigarette. "It is. The rest of what I told you, about the house fire and so forth, is all true."

"Why'd she do it?" Gabe repeated.

"No one knows," she said flatly. "After her husband died, Hester apparently began acting erratically. As I said, she wasn't seen in town often, but when she was seen, she was wearing the same long black dress she had worn to the funeral. Even in the summer, which, I don't have to tell you, was blisteringly hot, she wore the same long sleeves and high neck and full petticoat. She even refused to let little Celia go to school with the other children and wouldn't allow contact between her daughter and anyone. I suppose that once she lost her husband, she couldn't bear the thought of loosing another loved one. So she kept her close at all times."

Doris straightened her dress.

"I'd better get back to work now. My daughter..."

Don nodded in understanding. "We'd better get back to work as well. I can only play hooky for so long."

"Thank you for the information," said Gabe. "It certainly is interesting."

The old woman reached up and touched his cheek. "You seem like such a nice boy," she said. "It's a shame you're mixed up with that damnable house."

She turned and led the way back inside, adding loudly, "The next time you need maps, you might try city hall." She turned crisply to them. "Good day."

As they walked past, Katherine glowered, "Yes," she said with reserved anger. "And next time leave your cigarettes home."

CHAPTER 13

THE ATTIC DOOR CREAKED OPEN from the floor and fell with a calamitous bang on the rafters inside. As Trish peered into the darkness with her little flashlight, she couldn't help but wonder just what she thought she was doing, or would do if she found something.

With her daughters standing just outside the access door in the master bedroom, she tried to figure out why she had decided to put on a brave front when she was terrified. She wondered why had she climbed the rickety ladder into the dark attic instead of taking her family where they would be safe. The only answer she could come up with was that something was pulling her. Something simply insisted she know what was going on. There was something she simply had to see.

She played the beam from her flashlight around the cavernous room, jerking it over every time she thought she heard a noise. A scuttle here, a creak there, but nothing she could see could have possibly made such noise. She turned completely around on the ladder to see the other half of the attic. When the beam from her flashlight finally came to rest, her breath froze in her lungs. Sitting beneath the huge dormer in the side of the attic was an old rocking chair. It wasn't the chair itself that gave her a start, but that it was rocking softly in the narrow shafts of light.

"What is it mommy?" she barely heard, as if the voice was far away from her instead of just a few feet below.

Trish didn't answer. She slowly climbed fully into the attic and stood on the beams facing the chair.

"Mommy?" came Lizzy's voice, more concerned than frightened.

"Don't come up," she said. "Mommy will be right back."

Trish slowly crept along the beams watching the slow back and forth rhythm of the chair on the plywood platform. In the darkness, with only slivers of light to see her way, she was certain her eyes were beginning to play tricks on her, or did the dust indeed take shape and form into a wispy figure of a woman sitting in the chair? Did the darkness really seem to shift and ebb, as though clawing at the light in an attempt to snuff it out? Though the shadows moved around her, she was scarcely aware, her attention focused on the smoky figure that seemed unaware of, or at least uninterested in, her presence.

As she stepped from the beams to the platform, the rocking stopped, the figure grew still. Trish could feel her stomach knot, though could not tear herself from the place where she stood. The dust shifted as the figure turned to face her. Trish's flashlight fell and all went black.

LIZZY STOOD AT THE BASE OF THE LADDER clutching her sister. She could not believe her mother was up in the attic with who-knows-what and had left them there alone. She could feel her heart pounding in her temples. She'd only barely heard her mother warn her not to come up, as if she'd leave her sister alone in a house where she now knew no one was safe.

When she heard the sound of steps on the attic ladder, she whirled about, her muscles taut and ready to run from the house. She breathed relief when she saw her mother's sneakers on the rungs coming down. It wasn't until she saw her mother's face that she felt panic rise again.

There were tears running from her eyes, leaving traces in the dust on her face.

"Mommy?" she asked.

Trish said nothing, only stared straight ahead, her eyes unseeing, emotion running from their gaze. Lizzy put her sister down gently on the bed and crept to her mother's side. Trish sat on the bottom rung of the ladder, her hands clasped over her mouth.

"Horrible..." she said with quiet sorrow. "I saw it all. Horrible..."

Lizzy reached and touched her mother's face. Trish jerked at the contact and whirled about, as if unsure where she was.

"What..."

"Mommy? Are you okay?"

"Lizzy?" she asked. "What?"

"You're out of the attic. You were crying."

"Crying?" she asked incredulously. She dabbed her fingers under her eyes, finding them wet.

"Why?" asked Lizzy.

"I don't know," she said. "I honestly have no idea."

"Mom... you're really freaking me out," said Lizzy, steadying her mother as she rose shakily to her feet.

"I'm a little freaked out myself," she said. She scooped up her youngest daughter, who was playing happily on the bed, and walked to the kitchen. "My mouth is dry," she said. "I need some water."

In the kitchen, she put Shannon down in the middle of her toys where she could play quietly while Trish tried to sort out what had happened. Lizzy took a glass down from the cabinet, filled it with ice and water, and gave it to her mother. She took the empty stool across the island from her. Trish sipped the water thoughtfully, her head resting in her free hand.

"Mom," said Lizzy, her voice shaking. "Don't you remember anything about what happened up there?"

"I wish I did," she replied, her voice full of doubt and worry. "All I remember is walking up the ladder. There was a rocking chair. Then I found myself sitting back downstairs with you and your sister."

"Is that all?"

Her mother's eyes seemed to look for a thousand miles but only landed on the backside of her mind. "I remember... sadness. Profound sadness." As she said this, her body shuddered, as if the very mention of the word would drag her down into a melancholy from which the only release was death. She shook the feeling from her mind. "That's it. That's all I remember."

She took another sip of water. "What's happening here, Lizzy?" she asked. "What's happening to us?"

Lizzy looked as if she were struggling for words, although her mother didn't see.

"Mom," she said after a moment. "I've read all about this kind of thing."

"*What* kind of thing?" her mother asked, clearly exasperated.

"Everything that we're seeing is a sign of a classic haunting." She sounded every bit like an authority on the subject.

"There's no such thing..." Trish began, only to be cut off by her oldest.

"Really? Think about what we've seen," she said intently. "The shaking of the house, okay, was easily explained. But how do you explain us dreaming the same thing but from different points of view? And what just happened to you? And the footsteps and the cold wind and..." She paused, looking to her mother's clearly disbelieving expression. "And Shannon wasn't possessed," she said almost casually. "It's called Automatic Writing."

Her mother stared, as though unsure who or what this creature in front of her was. It certainly looked like her ten-year-old daughter, but she sounded like an expert in the paranormal world. Such a confident manner she rarely exhibited, only when she spoke or did something at which she really knew her business.

"How do you know..." she asked, her voice trailing off.

"Wait right here," she told her mother. "I'll show you." She bounded out of the room and into the house, returning moments later with several books in her arms. "You know those book-order-thingees that I keep getting from school?"

Trish looked at the titles: *The World of the Psychic; Ghosts, Witches, and Goblins: A Compendium of Things That go Bump in the Night; The World's Most Haunted Places;* and *The Ghost Hunter's Bible.*"

"I don't remember you ordering these," she said with a narrow glance and cocked eyebrow.

Lizzy grinned sheepishly. "That's because I changed the orders when I got to school."

"We'll talk about that later," said Trish, irritated and amused at the same time. "Tell me what you know. What's Auto..."

"Automatic Writing," said Lizzie, once again in authority mode. She opened one of her books and flipped to the appropriate page. "It's how a medium, or someone who is psychically sensitive, can talk to ghosts. They stare off into space while the ghost answers questions through them."

"And this is what's happening with your sister?"

Lizzy nodded. "It's what's happening to us all. This house is haunted."

Trish closed her eyes. "Then we're moving," she said, her voice full of defeat.

"Why?" Lizzy demanded. "Ghosts can't hurt us! I think it's cool!"

"I'm not raising your sister...or you...around ghosts. It's unhealthy."

"Fine," said Lizzy, snatching up her books. "Call Daddy again. Make us move again. I don't care." She stomped to her room and slammed the door hard, throwing herself on her bed. It wasn't fair.

CHAPTER 14

On the ride back to his office, Gabe said little. The sick feeling in his stomach was akin to the feeling that one must certainly get when realizing the train they've just boarded was lacking brakes. He sat, outwardly quiet, while the logical and spiritual sides of his mind waged an epic battle. Surely there were no such things as ghosts, but, if such beings did exist, his home certainly had history enough to invite them. But they did not exist.

There were rational explanations for everything that had happened in the house, though he might not be able to discover them himself. He was hardly even aware of Don's proclamations that seemed to grow in intensity as the street signs passed them. Not that he could have said something if he'd wanted to. He glanced up at his companion, who was spouting off statistics regarding hauntings and paranormal activities, one hand on the steering wheel, the other gesturing wildly.

"My dear boy," said Don with enthusiasm. "Do you realize what a treasure you may have stumbled onto? A real haunted house! Such things are more scarce than Dodo birds!"

"I don't believe in ghosts," said Gabe quietly.

"What?" he fairly cried as the car took a particularly fast corner.

"How can you not?"

"There has to be a logical explanation for what's happening at the house," said Gabe with determination. "Just because of a few rattling pipes and bad dreams, I'm not going to go running off about phantoms in the house."

They pulled into the parking lot beside Gabe's car.

"If you change your mind, let me know," said Don nonchalantly. "I'd love to do an investigation of the house."

"Sure," said Gabe as he slid out of his seat. "Thanks for the interesting afternoon."

"My pleasure," he beamed. "I'll take dinner as payment. Tomorrow night, yes? And I'll bring a lady friend."

Don waved cheerily as he pulled out of the parking space and sped off. Gabe waved back at him, trying to figure out how he'd given the impression that dinner would be a good idea.

Don was often prone to flights of fancy, especially with things dealing with the supernatural. Once he'd gone on an expedition in one of the more densely wooded areas of the surrounding area in search of Big Foot, stating later that the reason for his lack of findings was due to the rocky terrain of the Texas hill country making it damn near impossible to track anything.

But, in this case, there seemed to be more to his statements than mere sensationalistic interest. Don had, for as long as Gabe had known him, collected ghost stories and data about hauntings, had gone on ghost-hunts in Gettysburg and Massachusetts and had photographs from the famed Winchester mansion in California. This was the kind of thing none of his colleagues respected, but that Don knew a great deal about.

Gabe glanced at his watch. It was late enough in the day that going back to work seemed ridiculous. He fished in his pocket for his keys and a cigarette, got in his car, and headed home, all the while wondering in the back of his mind if Don might not just be right.

CHAPTER 15

"It's not fair," said Lizzy to Bishop as he yawned lazily on her pillow. "I don't want to move again, Bishop. I don't want to have to start over again. Not now. Not so soon."

Bishop's head snapped to attention, his eyes wide. He looked quickly around the room then leaped off the bed and hid underneath.

"Bishop?"

"No, it isn't fair."

Lizzy could barely hear the voice, a whisper, but could not tell from where it came. She whirled around, expecting to see her mother standing in the open doorway, but the door was still closed.

"Hello?" she asked timidly, the hairs on her neck beginning to prickle. She was suddenly aware that she was freezing.

"Not fair," came the whisper again.

Lizzy wrapped her blanket around her shoulders. Mom was afraid of ghosts, but she wasn't. She'd read everything she could about ghosts. They couldn't hurt you, so why should she be afraid of them? Once she'd gotten over being startled by the noises, she found herself quite intrigued and excited by the possibility of living with ghosts.

"Were you in my room last night?" she asked quietly. She didn't want her mother to hear her talking with a disembodied spirit. Mom would overreact, as usual, to anything she didn't understand, and they would move away for sure.

"Yes."

"Why?"

There was no answer. Lizzy strained her ears to hear even the slightest hint of a voice, but there was nothing to hear.

"Why?" she repeated with urgency. She turned as she heard her computer beep to life.

Creeping closer to the screen, she could see her art program start itself and pull up a blank canvas.

"Why were you in my room," she repeated to the screen, scarcely breathing as the electronic paintbrush began slowly to etch words on the white screen.

lonely

"Did you draw the picture?"

There was no answer.

"Did you draw the picture of us burning?" she demanded.

From all around her, the air seemed to shiver with quiet sobs. Lizzy looked at the screen where unseen hands had written *sorry*.

"Who are you?"

She watched as the paintbrush slowly made wide letters. It was a child's handwriting, as surely as if it were writing on the screen.

Celia. The unseen hand then drew little hearts and flowers around her name.

"Celia," began Lizzy. "Do you want us to leave?"

The canvas on the computer screen began to instantly fill with the word *no* repeated over and over again. Lizzy watched in astonishment as one after another electronic canvases filled with the word. She could feel her hair begin to prickle as she giggled nervously, her eyes wide with fascination.

"Okay, okay," she said softly. "What do you want?"

friend play stay

"We may not stay," replied Lizzy dejectedly. "My parents are really freaked out about all the weird stuff that's been going on."

nonononononononononononononono

"I'm sorry," she half-shouted, half-whispered. "They don't understand about... people like you. I do, though." She felt the air press around her like a cool blanket hugging her tight.

stay

Lizzy thought for a moment. Her parents would never understand. They never did. To them, her interests were either always dangerous or wrong or stupid or some other thing because they didn't understand it. For the first time since they'd moved to this house, she felt like she had a friend. She felt like someone wanted her around for more than just a convenient babysitter. She wasn't about to give that up easily.

"Give me some time to work on them," she said finally. "If you can keep from scaring them for a little while, I'm sure I can make them let us stay. Maybe if you talked to them the way you do to me..."

She was cut off by motion on the screen.

NO only you

"Why?" she asked, surprised. There was no answer forthcoming. "But maybe if they knew..."

NO

"Alright, then," she said. "Just me. A secret."

She felt the air hug tighter around her, then release and dissipate, gently scenting her room with the sweet smell of Oleander. Lizzy took a deep breath and smiled to herself. All of her anger had gone, and now she felt only the happiness that comes from meeting a new playmate.

She felt tired, and who wouldn't, she decided, after such an emotionally draining experience. Between her mother and her new friend, she decided she needed a nap. She crawled into her bed, pulled her blanket up around her, and smiled as she drifted into sleep. Daddy would be home in a little while, and she would get up for dinner, but for now, she just wanted to doze and imagine her new friend playing in the house that was now their charge.

CHAPTER 16

SHANNON SAT PLAYING QUIETLY in the large area adjacent to the kitchen, the strange little doll in the crook of her arm as if someone would steal it if she let it go. Her mother had, after she stopped shaking, changed her diaper then gone wearily back to the kitchen to start supper, never more than a second away from her.

As Trish rummaged through the refrigerator and cupboards, she couldn't help but glance over at her youngest, wondering what she must be making of all of this. Besides the most rudimentary of communication, a word here or there and babbling, she had no way of knowing what the toddler was thinking or feeling. She wished she knew if Shannon, too, felt the presence of something unnatural in the house.

If she did, she wasn't showing it at all, as she smiled and sang to herself and her strange little doll. She seemed happy, though not necessarily oblivious to what was going on. She reacted when her mother was upset, she seemed startled by the shaking and other phenomena, but she seemed to see them and accept them without any hesitation. How Trish wished she knew what she was thinking.

Lizzy, on the other hand, had no problem expressing herself, to the point of being precocious. Of course she knew all about what was going on. She always knew everything about everything, and damned be they who thought differently. At 10, nearly 11, years old, she was a typical adolescent girl, very opinionated and just as stubborn as her mother had been. Her behavior in the past couple of years had marked her hormonal changes with acts of rebellion and fits of temper.

This latest revelation about the book orders was just another in a long line of examples that Lizzy was trying to become an independent young woman. Still, Trish did not approve of such underhandedness. They'd have to have a long talk about it later.

She set the large casserole in the oven and turned back to the sink where vegetables were patiently waiting to be transformed into a salad. She broke the lettuce and sliced the tomatoes and radishes, threw them all into the large bowl on the counter and mixed them with her hands. As she reached for the bag of baby carrots, arms reached around her waist and hugged her tight. She screamed in surprise, jerking around and bringing her knee up hard, striking Gabe in the groin. He collapsed on the concrete floor.

"Oh my God! Are you alright?" she asked, fear and concern in her voice.

"Peachy," he replied weakly between gasps for air.

"You scared me! What the hell are you doing home? You're not supposed to be off for another fifteen minutes."

"Surprise," he said rolling onto his knees.

Trish helped him to his feet and kissed him lightly on the cheek.

"I'm sorry," she offered.

"My fault," he waved her off. "I shouldn't have scared you." The color in his face was returning to normal. "Goes along with the rest of my day. Are there any cold Cokes?"

Trish retrieved one out of the refrigerator and handed it to her husband who promptly sat on the stool with the chilled can resting firmly against his injured manhood. Trish giggled and turned back to the baby carrots.

"So what was wrong with the rest of your day?"

"Oh, let's see," he began. "First I debugged about a hundred lines of code, then I spent my lunch hour at the Historical Society only to be treated like crap and told that there was no money to help redo the house..."

"They do that?"

"Apparently not anymore," he said with much irritation. "Then I got to hear a wonderfully macabre yarn about the house and how some crazy woman burned herself and her daughter to death in it."

He didn't notice how Trish flinched when he mentioned the burning house or the woman. "Then all the way back to my office Don went on about haunted houses..."

"Don?"

"Thorndyke. You remember him, right? He sent me over there to begin with. Turns out he knows the old lady at the Society and she finally talked to me when she found out I was his friend. Anyways, he's convinced this house is ripe for a haunting and wants to do a full investigation on it. Oh, and he's also coming for dinner tomorrow night, with a date no less."

"A date? What am I supposed to cook?"

"I don't know. I'm sure you'll think of something. You're a wonderful cook. Then I came home and wanted to sneak up behind my wife and give her a romantic little kiss on the cheek, but got kneed in the balls for my efforts. How was your day?"

Trish smiled weakly. "Fine," she said, adding, "I think. Seems like something happened today." Her brow wrinkled as she tried to remember what it was that was so important to tell her husband. Something had happened, but the more she tried to remember what it was, the more elusive the memory of the event became. "I can't remember what. I remember hearing something in the living room. Like footsteps. They went up into the attic."

"Were they the same kind of noises we've heard before?"

"I think so, but these were more like footsteps than banging pipes. Running footsteps. Then they went up into the attic above our room." At the mention of the attic, she felt immediately fearful, but could not remember why. "That's all I can remember. Gabe, do you think this house might really be haunted?"

"Don't be silly," he snorted. "You're starting to sound like Don. This is a really old house, and I'm sure it's just settling. There's no such thing as ghosts." He opened his drink and took a long appreciative sip. "So where are the girls?" he asked at last.

"Well, Lizzy is in her room, pissed off about something, as usual. And Shannon is..." Her voice trailed off in the realization that the toddler was no longer sitting where Trish had left her. Again, the feeling of dread seized her insides. "Where'd she go?" she asked as she bounded around the island. "Shannon?" she called.

She rounded the corner into the dining room with Gabe hobbling after her. "Shannon!" she called louder. She couldn't have gotten very far. Trish cursed at herself for not being more attentive. What if she was hurt? What if she'd gotten locked in a closet? What if she'd fallen down the stairwell to the unfinished basement? Trish looked down the stairs into the inky blackness. "Shannon?" she called again. She turned to Gabe. "Can you check down there while I check her room?"

He nodded and started painfully down the stairs, calling his daughter's name on the way. Trish crossed the room to Shannon's closed door. She stopped and listened at the door, sighing in relief as she heard familiar babbling and the toddler's distinctive belly laugh from inside.

"Gabe! She's up here!" she called out to her husband. She opened the door to the room and, sure enough, there sat Shannon, grinning and clutching the strange little doll.

"Hi Mommy!" she beamed.

"Hi baby. You scared Mommy, running off like that."

Shannon giggled and rushed to hug her mother around the knees. Trish paused to look around Shannon's room. It looked the same as it had, save that the little people that belonged in her dollhouse were all standing up in a row looking at where Shannon had been sitting. She picked Shannon up and closed the door behind them as they left the room. "C'mon," she said. "Dinner is almost ready."

She turned in time to see Gabe coming up the stairs.

"I'm building a gate for this stairwell," he said. "It just occurred to me that one of the kids, or us, could fall down those things."

"Good idea," said Trish, still hugging Shannon tight. "Lizzy!" she called out. "Dinner!"

They went back into the kitchen and, while Gabe cleared the little table they ate, Trish put Shannon in her high chair and got down dishes.

"Lizzy," she called again. "Come set the table!"

After a few moments of no response, she sighed heavily. "Would you get our oldest and drag her in here for dinner?" she asked Gabe. He nodded and limped out toward Lizzy's room.

As he crossed the living room and made his way toward her door, he couldn't help but wonder what it was that she was upset about this time. Where she and her mother was concerned, even the smallest of points could be blown up into a full-scale battle.

It almost always came down to him listening to both sides of the argument and acting as an impartial moderator to come up with some sort of compromise that let Trish have the feeling she was the parent, and therefore the authority figure, and Lizzy the feeling she was allowed to be her own person and was somewhat independent. It was not that he liked the role; he just wanted there to be peace in the home and for the family to get along with one another. Though Lizzy and Trish loved each other dearly, they often fought as if the case were otherwise.

He knocked on her door, a practice she'd insisted on as she was growing up and needed her privacy.

"Lizzy?" he called. There was no answer.

He gingerly opened the door, feeling a start as the black and white blur that was Bishop streaked past him. Peering inside, he saw her curled up under her blanket on her bed. The room, he noticed, was very cold.

"Lizzy," he called softly, not wanting to startle her awake. She did not move, only continued snoring softly. He crept inside and next to her bed. He shook her softly.

"Lizzy."

She sat bolt upright in her bed and whirled around, eyes wide.

"WHAT!?" She blinked at her father. "Hi, Daddy."

"Um, It's dinner time. Your mother needs you to help her set the table."

She groaned in protest as she got up, another habit she'd developed in the past few years. It was her way of telling anyone within earshot that whatever you asked her to do, you were greatly inconveniencing her.

"Something wrong, pumpkin?" he asked, ignoring her attitude.

"I was asleep," she snapped.

"It's five o'clock in the afternoon. A little late for taking a nap, isn't it?"

She huffed in reply. Although he didn't like her manner at the moment, he decided now was not the best time to scold her for it. He, himself, was known to be a little grumpy on first getting up. Instead, he changed the subject.

"You want to tell me what you're mad at your mother for?"

"Nothing," she said dejectedly. "It's just that Mom wants to move. She says she doesn't like being in a haunted house."

There's that word again, thought Gabe. "This house is not haunted," he said forcefully. "There's no such thing as a haunted house, ghosts, or anything of the like, and I'm sick of hearing about it."

For the briefest of moments, Lizzy wanted to tell him that, yes, the house was haunted, and the spirit of Celia was her friend, but a voice in the back of her mind stopped her. *They won't believe you, it said. They won't understand. They'll just think you're making it up for attention. Don't tell. It's our secret.* She let the matter drop as she shuffled to the door.

"Besides," continued Gabe, "we couldn't move even if we wanted to right now. We're not going anywhere."

His last statement seemed to lift her spirits just a bit, and she put her arm around him as they left her room. By the time they got to the kitchen, Trish was pulling the casserole out of the oven.

"Oh good," she said seeing them. "Lizzy, you can put ice in the glasses. Gabe, come dish up a plate for Shannon."

Gabe and Lizzy looked at each other. Gabe grinned. "Yes, General Mom, Ma'am," he bellowed while saluting.

Trish shot him a look of mock-irritation and threw a dishcloth at him as he and Lizzy got to work with their respective duties. When all was done, they dished up their own plates and sat in their usual places at the table. After the blessing was said, dinner was underway. Trish had cooked something consisting of potatoes and cheese, hamburger meat and spices of one sort or another. Once again, thought Gabe, she's turned a limited budget and near-empty pantry into a meal fit for a king.

Conversation throughout the meal was mostly cordial, with nothing being said of ghosts or phenomena, and Trish, for one, was glad of it. It bothered her that she couldn't remember the events of the afternoon, and could not figure out why exactly she felt sure they needed to leave the house. Whatever the cause of it, with her husband making light conversation and the children eating peacefully, she could almost forget about the worries on her mind. She was thankful the meal went by without a cross word, a sideways glance, or even a tossed morsel from Shannon. It was nice.

Once dinner was done, Shannon and Lizzy went to the bathroom to take a shower, leaving Gabe and Trish to tidy up. They stacked the dirty crockery in the dish washer and waited to hear the water from the bathroom running before stepping outside to smoke.

"So Lizzy tells me you want us to move again," said Gabe, taking a long draw on his cigarette.

Trish blew smoke out her nose. "I got scared. I don't know why." Why couldn't she remember?

"Because you realize we can't move, right?" Gabe was being patronizing, a trait that made Trish want to strangle him, especially when he was right.

"I know," she said tersely.

"Was that it?" he asked. "Or was there something else she was mad about."

"I don't know. Who can tell with her anymore?" She took another drag off her cigarette. "So tell me this yarn about the house. You said someone died here?"

"Yeah. Apparently, a woman burned herself and her daughter to death in this house."

"Wow," she said, surprised but otherwise unaffected by the revelation.

"Yeah. It gets weirder." It took him the rest of his cigarette and half of another to relate the entire story, the best he could recall it. Trish sat with fascination until he was done.

"How sad," she said at last, staring at the glowing end of her cigarette.

They went back inside and finished tidying the kitchen. Gabe went to lay out his clothes for the next day and iron a shirt, while Trish collected the children from the shower. It had been a running joke between them that it was their children, and not the hot Texas sun, that caused the drought every year. As he put the finishing creases on the sleeves of his favorite olive shirt, Trish walked past, Shannon bundled in a towel in her arms, Lizzy following, to the bathroom for the evening ritual of brushing and drying tangled nests of hair.

"I'm taking the garbage out," he called after them. He put his shirt on a hanger, which he placed on a doorknob, and went to the kitchen to pull the overflowing trash bag from the can. As he hauled it out the door and up the stairs to the garage, he fished in his pocket for another cigarette. Although the trash did need to be taken out, he really just wanted a moment without the family to reflect by himself. He dumped the bag into the large bin outside the garage and sat down on a conveniently placed box, lighting his cigarette.

It was his intention to stay positive. After everything his family had been through, moving twice in one year, Trish losing her job, filing bankruptcy, he'd simply decided after a fit of depression that he was no good to anyone if he didn't put forward a cool demeanor. The fact of the matter was he was terrified and morose over their current situation, but he was beginning to feel a little hopeful.

He'd done his best to hide his newly-developed ulcer from his wife, no easy task considering her cooking habits, by eating antacids constantly throughout the day. He was also painfully conscious of how he spoke to his children.

Time was, before all of their financial woes, that Lizzy's huffing and puffing over being asked to do a simple task such as setting the dinner table would have set him off on a tirade. Now, not wishing to add to anyone's problems, he kept his emotions bottled up inside him, taking release whenever he could through physical labor, or smoking.

But now there was a new problem: the house, or something in it. While he still did not believe it was haunted, he could not deny that there was something amiss. He saw it whenever he looked at his wife. She was a very beautiful woman, but now she wore an expression of tired sadness he couldn't bear. Her usually easy-going attitude had been replaced by an uneasiness that, in his opinion, bordered on paranoia.

He felt a tear roll down his cheek as he took a long draw off his cigarette, and he instinctively wiped it away. Must stay strong, he told himself. Can't let the family down.

Trish had been uneasy since they came into the house, and now she was seeing and hearing things. Phantom shadows in the shower and giants walking across the living room were the kind of things he believed could not happen, or were just tricks of light and creaking boards. She, however, seemed to place more stock in them, and it worried him.

But then, he thought, as the burning sensation in his stomach began to gain strength, what if she were not hallucinating? He drew in a lungful of smoke and ground his teeth defiantly against the pain in his gut, fighting it back down until it had subsided. What if there were something in the house? What then?

They certainly could not leave. They had no place to go, and no means to get one. No, this house was their best and only hope of putting their lives back together, and it was here they would stay. But what to do? That was the question. He did not know how much longer he could continue treating his wife with kid gloves before losing his temper. He had only so much good humor to go around, and keeping the family's spirits up seemed to take most of it.

The sound of the door that led back into the house startled him into quickly standing like a child who'd just been caught.

"Taking out the garbage, huh?" Trish said teasingly.

Gabe kicked his feet and looked guiltily at the burned out cigarette butt in his hand. "I took it out," he said sheepishly.

"Uh-huh," she smiled as she turned and went back down the stairs to the kitchen. He deposited the butt in the dumpster and pressed the button to close the garage door. She wasn't crazy, he thought. She still had the same warm sense of humor he'd fallen in love with years ago.

As he watched the heavy door slowly obscure the outside, he had a curious feeling of being trapped, of wanting to dive through the ever-narrowing gap into the freedom that the night air promised. He shook his head and walked back down the stairs, turning off the garage light behind him, and closed the door. He glanced at his watch. How did it get to be so late? he wondered. It was already nine o'clock, and he had work in the morning. It was time to put the girls to bed and spend some time with Trish.

Gabe walked back through the door into the kitchen to find Lizzy waiting for him, hair wet and braided in a long pony tail.

"Good night, Daddy," she said, reaching up to hug his neck and kiss him. "Thank you for letting us stay," she whispered in his ear. "I really love it here."

He kissed her forehead. "I'm glad, pumpkin."

With that, she bounded off to her room, oddly excited, he decided, to be going to bed. Normally it was a fight to get to stay up till all hours of the morning. As she disappeared through the doorway, humming some strange little song, he shook his head in amazement.

He crossed the kitchen and went toward Shannon's room where, he could tell by the soft humming coming through the empty flue over the door, Trish was putting her to bed. He quietly opened the door and stood, smiling broadly at the sight of his wife and youngest child.

He always admired the way Trish dealt with the kids. She always told him she was good with them because of her many brothers and sisters, because she'd had to babysit them most of her life, but that was not it at all. Gabe felt the reason that she was so good at it was because she was born to do it. At her very core, she was a natural mother. True, she was a wife, lover, best friend, and other things. But the thing that set her apart from any other woman he'd ever met was that she seemed born to care for their children, and she loved doing it.

Trish was pulling the blanket up around Shannon, tickling her and touching her face lovingly. It made Gabe's heart feel lighter, as if all the problems he was worrying about were almost nonexistent. Trish finally got up and, gesturing for him to be quiet, left the room with Gabe, closing the door behind them.

"She's so cute," she said softly. She turned to face Gabe. "Could you please check the air-conditioning filter?" she asked. "It's pretty warm in there."

"Really?" he said. He poked his head silently back into Shannon's room. She was already drifting off to sleep. Trish was right; it was warm in the room. It wasn't hot, but it was warm enough to be noticed. He withdrew his head and softly closed the door.

"I'll have a look at it as soon as I can," he replied cheerily.

Together they went across the living room to Lizzy's room. Light still could be seen over the door. Gabe knocked.

"Come in," came the familiar reply.

As they stepped over the threshold of the room, they both shivered. Where Shannon's room had been a toasty warm, Lizzy's room was by far the coldest room in the house.

"Lights out," said Trish authoritatively. Lizzy huffed in compliance.

"Hey, what'cha reading there?" asked Gabe as he picked up the book his oldest had just put down on her night table. *Ghosts, Witches, and Goblins: A Compendium of Things that Go Bump in the Night.* "Where'd you get this?" he asked, not bothering to try to conceal the edge to his voice.

"We'll talk about it later," said Trish quickly before Lizzy could stammer a reply. She bent and kissed her daughter on the cheek. "Goodnight, sweetheart."

Gabe eyed her suspiciously as she breezed out of the room. He hated not knowing what was going on, but they'd evidently discussed the matter beforehand, and his input was neither necessary nor wanted. It made him bristle. He kissed Lizzy on top of her head.

"Goodnight, pumpkin," he said. Then, holding up the book, he added "Mind if I borrow this for a while?"

"Go ahead," said Lizzy sleepily.

As he left the room and closed the door, she snuggled into her pillow and smiled softly as unseen hands brushed her hair away from her face.

"Goodnight," came the whispered voice.

"Goodnight, Celia," mumbled Lizzy as she drifted off into slumber.

IN THE WARMTH OF HER ROOM, Shannon lay clutching the strange little poppet with one hand, her bottle in the other, drifting lazily in and out of sleep. She didn't seem to mind the shadows that drifted about the room, almost taking shape, but never achieving substance. Between extended blinks, she saw the shadows unplug the transmitter to the monitor, though she didn't know what significance it had.

They were her friends, the shadows. It was in their warmth that she'd found her doll. It was in their darkness she'd heard the whispered singing that brought her comfort. At two years old, she could not comprehend the words to the lullaby, but knew of the happiness she felt when she heard it.

The shadows moved slowly, blending with some and pulling out of others, until they rested in the folding rocking chair Trish had set up beside the bed and began rocking softly back and forth.

"Hush now, little angel," they whispered with a hundred voices of bells. "Sleep now."

Shannon smiled, hugging her doll and bottle close when she heard the familiar little tune lightly filtering through the air, and soon she too was asleep.

CHAPTER 17

TIME PASSED QUICKLY FOR GABE THE NEXT DAY. Work was steady, though not overwhelmingly so, which was the way he liked it. Such a schedule did not allow him time to brood over the previous day's events, nor did it give him time to worry. By the time he got off work, he was mentally exhausted. Just before he left, Don popped by his office for a cheery hello and a brief reminder he and his mystery date would be coming for dinner.

By the time he got home, Trish was already cooking something he was sure would taste every bit as divine as it smelled. The scent told him he was not needed in the kitchen, so he set to work cleaning up the clutter that only children can bring. He roused Lizzy, who was sleeping again, and together they quickly put away toys and shoes.

Although the mess didn't seem too terribly large, it took them longer than he thought it would to put it all away. He took a handful of toys to Shannon's room, then went back for a stack of bills that needed to be put in his room. He came back, only to find what appeared to be the same toys he'd just put away neatly piled in the middle of the room.

"Very funny, Lizzy," he chided. "We have guests coming and we don't have time for screwing around."

"What?" she demanded.

"The toys. Did you just bring them back out here?"

"No."

Despite her tone, Gabe could see she was telling the truth. He shook his head. Maybe he was more tired than he thought. Maybe he only thought those were the same toys. After all, many of them did look alike. He decided he was mistaken and continued cleaning.

It took him all of an hour to straighten the house sufficiently, and by the time he put the last of the clutter in a convenient hiding place, there was a knock at the back door.

"Good evening!" Don beamed as Trish opened the door. "Thanks for having us over. This is my friend Elenor."

"Call me Nell, please," she said. She was a slight woman, easily 20 years Don's junior, with shoulder-length auburn hair and large round eyes that seemed to take in the entire room at once. She seemed somewhat shy, but friendly. She shook Trish's hand and then Gabe's as she crossed the threshold into the house.

"Dinner's almost ready," said Trish cheerily as she went back to her cooking. "It shouldn't take more than a few minutes."

"Fine," said Don. "That means Gabe can give us a tour of the house, yes?"

Gabe nodded and led the way further into the house. As they crossed into the dining room, he noticed that Elenor seemed to flinch and shoot a look of panic at Don, who smiled and nodded at her.

"Well," he began. "The kitchen you've already seen; this is the dining room. The door to the right is Shannon's room."

"Shannon?" asked Elenor.

As if on cue, the toddler came running around the corner and hugged her daddy's knees hard. Gabe felt lucky every time she did this, not only because it showed how much she loved him, but also because she didn't weigh just a few pounds more, or she might actually hurt him.

"This," he said scooping her up, "is my youngest daughter, Shannon. Shannon, can you say hello to Don and Nell?"

"Hi," she said shyly, and buried her face against her father's neck.

"Hello, Shannon," said Elenor.

Shannon wiggled in her way to let Gabe know she wanted down and ran off to the kitchen and her mother. Elenor watched her go with wide eyes and a wondrous expression.

"She's beautiful," she said to Gabe.

He was used to such comments about his children. Hardly a day went by without someone telling him how wonderful his children were, and though they obviously got their beauty from their mother, he still felt pride whenever he heard such things.

"Thank you," he said. "The door to the right is Trish and my room."

"Can we see?" asked Don.

"Pardon the mess," Gabe shrugged as he opened the door. The room was in a state of disarray, though his guests didn't seem to mind. As they entered the room, Gabe noticed Elenor nodding almost imperceptibly to Don. He also noticed Don smiling and fidgeting with some unseen item in his hand. It began to come clear to Gabe that there was more to this visit than just dinner.

"The bathroom is interesting," he said with forced politeness. He hated being played, and although he was not truly angry with Don for the deception, he did want to know just what was going on. "The previous owners started remodeling in here and never finished."

"A hot tub?" Don was clearly as surprised as Gabe and Toby had been at the discovery.

"Yup."

"Weird."

Without another word they turned and made their way back through the bedroom, pausing for a moment as Don noticed the door that was a full two feet off the ground.

"Where does that go?" he asked.

"The attic. We haven't really been up there yet. It's just another in the long list of things that has to be done in this house."

"And where do these stairs go?" asked Don as they exited the bedroom.

"That's the unfinished basement. It looks like a disaster area down there."

"May we see it?" Don was clearly intrigued by that area of the house, and Gabe was beginning to suspect why.

"I guess so," he said uneasily.

"May I borrow your bathroom?" asked Elenor hastily, seizing Don's arm. Her eyes never left the stairwell.

"Sure," said Gabe. "Do you want us to wait for you to go down?"

She shook her head vigorously. "I don't want to go down there," she said quickly. "I mean, it's dark and there's probably nothing we can really see in the dark, right?" Her worried expression fixed on Don's eyes, but he smiled back at her.

"We'll be back up in a jiffy, then," he said as she disappeared into the bathroom and closed the door.

At the bottom of the stairwell, Gabe unlocked the heavy door and pushed, its hinges squeaking in protest. Beyond the light that reached from the top of the stairs, all was blackness.

"Creepy," muttered Don, eliciting a surprised and quizzical look from Gabe.

"You want to tell me what's really going on here?" he asked after a moment.

"Whatever could you mean?" Don replied with mock innocence.

"You know damned well what I mean. What are you guys really doing here? And who is she? She's young enough to be your daughter."

Don sighed. "Nell is one of the most gifted mediums that I've ever had the privilege of working with. I just wanted to check out your house, that's all. I mean, after the story we heard yesterday, I couldn't resist, and I didn't want to upset or startle anyone. It just seemed the best way was to invite myself over for dinner."

"You know I don't believe in that stuff," Gabe said, his voice dripping with exasperation. "And I don't want Trish to be upset."

"I promise, no one will be the wiser."

"And what the hell are you fumbling with in your pocket?"

Don looked embarrassed for a moment, as though he had been caught with his fingers in the icing. From his pocket he pulled a small gray box with a window on it.

"It's a Gaussmeter," he said sheepishly. "It's designed for measuring electromagnetic energy."

Gabe shook his head. "You amaze me."

"My dear boy, I come from a long line of misunderstood people."

At the top of the stairs stood Elenor looking apprehensive. As they closed the door to the basement, her expression eased a bit, though it was still apparent that she was nervous about something. As they reached the top of the stairs, Don gave a conspiratory glance to Elenor.

"The jig is up," he said with a sheepish grin. "He knows what we're doing here."

"Good," replied Elenor. "Because there's such a presence..."

"I don't want to know," Gabe cut in with a hushed whisper. "Look, you believe in what you want, but I don't believe in ghosts, hauntings, monsters, or any other thing that would upset my wife and kids. So as far as this evening is concerned, you two are here for dinner. Right?"

The look on his face let them know he was serious, and challenging him would be futile. They nodded their agreement.

"Dinner's ready!" called Trish from the kitchen. Gabe gave them both a look of warning before they went to eat.

Trish had prepared a dinner of spaghetti and meatballs with garlic bread and a garden salad. The aroma of basil and garlic wafted through the air in a tempting haze. As they sat down, Lizzy, who had been strangely out of view for most of the evening, emerged from her room and joined them to eat.

"You must be Lizzy," said Elenor. "You're quite the pretty young lady."

Lizzy gave a half-hearted smile and sat down.

The rest of the meal was eaten amid small talk about their respective jobs (Elenor apparently was a librarian in her working hours) and how lovely the old house would be once it was finished. Shannon covered herself from head to foot with sticky red spaghetti sauce, an action which further endeared herself to Elenor and Don, while Lizzy said nothing, only sat with the same annoyed expression and pouting frown.

When dinner was finished, Don and Elenor excused themselves from coffee, stating that they both had to work in the morning. They bid the family a fond goodnight and made their way back to Don's car by way of the terra-cotta patio.

They got into the car in silence. Elenor wore a look of genuine fear and pain. She didn't seem to relax at all until the car was pulling away from the house with high pillars. At long last, she finally turned to Don.

"You son-of-a-bitch," she said.

"What?"

"You didn't tell me what kind of thing is in that house."

"I didn't know…"

"You will never get me back into that damned house again. You can't make me go back in."

"Nell, I'm sorry. I didn't know."

She said nothing for the rest of the ride home, and aside from the occasional rubbing of her arms as though trying to warm herself, she scarcely moved. Don wanted to say something, anything, to better the situation, but there were no words that could repair the damage he had done.

CHAPTER 18

TRISH PASSED THROUGH THE DARKENED HOUSE, painfully aware of how quiet it was. The boards of the hardwood floor were cold on her bare feet as she stepped silently from one pool of moonlight to the next.

The house was different somehow, but she could not place the inconsistencies. It seemed smaller, older. Yet here she was in same living room adjacent to her oldest daughter's room, admiring the Victorian loveseat that, though she knew did not belong to her, seemed perfectly natural under the large front room window.

The realization that the couch was not hers gave rise to the observation that, in fact, nothing in the room was hers. Where her television had been, a spinet now sat quietly. The piles of boxes that still awaited unpacking were nowhere to be found, replaced by dark, richly wooded end tables, which surrounded chairs of the same ornate brocade fashion as the loveseat.

Still, none of this seemed to bother her. None of the fineries in this room seemed out of place. It was as if they had been there all along, unseen but present all the same. Through the branches of the myrtle outside the window, she watched the dawn sky lighten in hue to a paler blue and then leap to life with vibrant reds and pinks heralding the sun's arrival.

Such beauty, she thought, must be shared. She turned toward Lizzy's door and stopped. Where the rest of the house was in a beautiful state, her door was in a state of decay. Wood flaked off and slimy bits encrusted the crevices left behind. The pungent scent of rot wafted from the door, causing Trish to retreat a few steps.

Before she could advance on the door to investigate further, the knob rattled, turned from the inside. As the strings of sticky muck that tried to hold the door to the frame broke, the air went cold, chilling Trish to the bone. She could not tear her eyes away from the doorframe as a small figure came into her presence.

It was a little girl, no more than ten, with ringlets of strawberry blonde and eyes that shimmered green in the morning light. She had a cherubic face that held only kindness and love in its countenance.

"Hello, little girl," said Trish as she bent down, her own voice sounding as though it were poorly dubbed. "What's your name?"

The little girl giggled and walked toward Trish, arms held wide.

"Where's your mommy?" she asked taking the child in her embrace. The little girl was cold to the touch, making Trish pull away slightly.

"You're my mommy now," said the angelic face as it twisted into a smile of madness. Trish barely caught sight of the straight razor gleaming in the sunlight as the child brought it quickly toward Trish's throat.

"No!" she screamed, sitting up and gasping for breath. The little girl's laugh echoed through her mind, and for a moment, Trish thought she could see her giggling at the foot of her bed, the razor dripping with deep crimson. Her eyes darted around the still darkened room as recognition began to sink in. She'd dreamed it. It was another goddamned dream. She could hear her heart beating in her ears and felt the cool wind of the ceiling fan. She looked over at Gabe, who was sleeping still.

She slid quietly out of bed and felt for her house shoes, finding the padded terrycloth comforting. She moved as quietly as she could to the bathroom, turning on the light only after she had closed the door behind her. Once inside, she went to the far mirror, turned on the cold water and began vigorously splashing her face. As the water pooled in her hands, she realized how badly she was shaking. With each new splash of water, the dream faded until it was only a hazy memory at best.

She knew she'd had a bad dream, but as had the others before it; this one was vanishing. Now the dream was as much as smoke, but she could not reason why she could not stop her hands shaking. All that remained of the dream were the feelings of dread and panic. And the face, the angelic face that for some reason she could not remember, sent chills down her spine.

She splashed her face again and looked up to get a towel. For the briefest of moments, she could have sworn she saw the child here, just as surely as she had in her dream, staring back at her, reflected in the mirror. Trish whirled around, looking for the child, but found no one.

With her heart still pounding and all of her senses violently alert, she realized that attempting to go back to sleep would be futile and would probably only succeed in waking her husband. She turned off the bathroom light, feeling a twinge of fear as she was plunged into darkness, and exited the bathroom, glancing at the clock on the way out to the kitchen. It was nearing 5:00 a.m., only an hour before Gabe had to get up for his morning ritual of preparing for work.

While it was usually his custom to leave her sleeping, waking her only for a kiss goodbye, today, she decided, she'd surprise him and have breakfast ready by the time he got up. It was Friday, after all, and she could always get a nap in later, if Shannon cooperated, and if her nerves settled down.

CHAPTER 19

A PLEASANT MORNING WENT A LONG WAY for Gabriel, in that it made for a good mood and set him toward a good day. Mornings in his home were routinely less than serene, as he often overslept just long enough to give his heart a start when he finally did open his eyes and look at the clock. From there, it was a hurried, but thorough shower, dressing frantically, stealing a kiss from his sleeping wife, and grabbing at a travel-mug of coffee as he raced out the door. Somehow, he always managed to make it to work on time, though he always felt as if he were running late.

This morning, however, had been quite different. To begin with, he'd been awakened by the smell of cooking bacon. The delicious aroma gently lifted him out of sleep a few minutes before his alarm was to sound, so he went ahead and got up. A relatively lazy shower later, he emerged from the bedroom dressed and feeling anything but hurried this morning. He had found his wife in the kitchen cooking pancakes with a plate full of bacon next to her. When they'd first gotten married, she'd often made him breakfast and saw him out the door, but that was when he worked construction at his father's site and they had not needed for her to get a job. Life, it seemed, had just gotten in the way.

They'd eaten breakfast and she'd kissed him goodbye and he'd left, feeling every bit like today would be a good day, and things were going to get better for them. The drive to work had been uneventful, and he'd even found a parking place in front of his building, a thing coveted by all his colleagues. Now at work, he settled into his chair and began his day of delivering equipment, updating web sites, and solving "emergencies" for the faculty and students of the University, all with an easy feeling that could only be brought about by such a morning.

He stepped out of his office for a cup of coffee in the little hidden kitchen off the mail room. When he returned, he found the familiar screen alerting him to his more than forty e-mail messages. Though most of them were unsolicited advertisements of some sort or another, one in the list caught his attention.

Gabe,

Hey guy...Thought you might find this interesting. Anything sound vaguely familiar?

D

Attached to the message was an article about haunted houses and ways to tell if your house was haunted.

Gabe closed the message without reading the article beyond the title, chuckling to himself about Don's eccentricities. He left the message in his computer, for future amusement, and went about his day. By noon, the article was mostly forgotten in a haze of computer code and wires that took his attention. He ate lunch alone at his desk, as was his custom, while still keeping to the arduous task of updating files. By the end of the day, he was again mentally exhausted, but still happy thanks to Trish's efforts that morning.

He returned home that evening to find Trish in the kitchen, looking tired, but smiling as Shannon played at her feet. Lizzy was outside in the little playhouse singing quietly to no one in particular and making conversation with some imaginary playmate. It seemed the closest thing to picture-perfect family life that Gabe had seen in a very long time, and it only made his mood better.

As the door closed behind him, Trish looked up and smiled.

"Good timing," she said. "Dinner's almost ready. Get Lizzy to help you set the table."

Gabe set the satchel he laughingly referred to as a briefcase in the old leather easy chair on his way back out the door.

"Lizzy!" he called. "Dinner time!"

He was slightly startled by her appearance as she emerged from the playhouse. It wasn't her expression, all smiles and joy, that bothered him. Rather, the fact she looked pale, sickly and drawn gave him cause for worry. Her usually tan and rosy cheeks were faded somehow. Bags under her eyes made her look ten years older.

"Honey," he asked, his voice full of concern. "Are you feeling okay?"

"I'm fine, Daddy," she said dismissively. "I'm just a little tired, that's all."

"Are you sleeping alright?"

"I guess so," she said with a shrug. "Just not enough."

She brushed past him into the house where the smell of Trish's Yankee pot roast was a welcome indulgence. Together they set the table and filled the glasses while Trish put Shannon in her high chair and set out steaming bowls of vegetables. Then they gathered around the table and said a brief blessing before beginning the repast.

Dinner was taken with little conversation. Gabe's inquiries about how everyone's day had been and the most cursory of answers was all that broke the relative silence of chewing and swallows. When they had all finished, Lizzy helped clear the table while Trish wiped Shannon's hands and Gabe put the leftover food away. The children were sent to take showers and Trish and Gabe sat out on the terra-cotta patio smoking.

"I'm worried about Lizzy," said Gabe once they had sat down. "She doesn't look well."

Trish sipped her tea and took a long drag off her cigarette. "Oh?" she said distractedly.

"You too," he added. "You both look very tired."

"I just haven't been sleeping well," she said. "Bad dreams."

"About what?" The admission of nightmares had piqued his interest.

"I can't remember," she said staring at the glowing end of her cigarette. "Something to do with fire, but I can't remember what."

"Maybe you should make an appointment for both of you to see a doctor," he offered.

"I'm fine," she cut back. "I'll take Lizzy in to see the doctor tomorrow, but I'm fine."

Gabe knew by the tone of her voice that it was her final word on the subject. When she decided there was a serious problem, she would go on her own. Her own will, however, would not let her go for something she deemed minor.

They finished smoking and went inside, Trish to fetch the girls from the shower, Gabe to the table, notebook in hand, to plan out the work for tomorrow. Saturday was no longer a day of rest for him, as there was much to do to make the house suitable for his family.

He'd already arranged for Toby to come with his truck so they could get lumbar and plywood to fix the front porch. Now he was making a list of the tools and materials he would need. His parents had left a credit card with a high limit for him to use in the repair of the house, the expense of which was to be added to the loan from Gabe's parents, and it was his intention to be as meticulous as possible with keeping records of how every penny was spent.

By the time he was done for the evening, his list contained five full sheets of three-quarter inch plywood, several yards worth of trim, gray primer, white paint, wood putty, screws, an electric sander, and various other items he deemed were necessary.

"Tell your father goodnight."

He looked up to see his children standing beside his chair, clean and beautiful in their pajamas. He looked around to the clock, realizing for the first time that he'd been so absorbed in the planning that he'd completely lost track of time. He'd spent nearly two hours writing, planning, rewriting and such.

He hugged and kissed them each and then watched as Lizzy trudged off to her room and Trish carried Shannon to her bed. He couldn't help but feel a little pride at seeing them, such good girls, and their mother.

He sighed and went back to his notebook, checked his figures one last time, then closed it as Trish walked into the room and slumped down into the easy chair with a great huff of exhaustion. He got up and kissed the top of her head as she picked up the remote control and flipped through the channels.

He took his place on the couch and they sat for a while, neither really interested in the programs the television offered. After a while, she came and lay down on the couch, resting her head in his lap. He sat stroking her hair gently as she snuggled closer to him. As the images flickered on the television screen, she seemed to him almost asleep save for her weary eyes that would not close.

He was worried for her. Whatever kind of stress she was under was clearly taking its toll. She had woken up several nights to dreams, but she could not, or would not, tell him what they were about. Apart from her apparent state of exhaustion, she seemed fine. Perhaps in a few weeks she would begin to relax, get her bearings. Perhaps then she could look for work. Perhaps then she could sleep.

"I'm going to bed," he said. "Long day tomorrow. Sarah is bringing Zach and Vincent for the kids to play with."

"Maybe Sunday I'll get some sleep," she sighed as she followed him to the bedroom.

CHAPTER 20

In the darkness of Lizzy's room, Bishop's eyes glowed wide and fearful from his spot under the desk. He growled deep in his throat as the cold shadows snaked across the room to his sleeping mistress's bed. He watched as they settled over her body and descended upon her, seeming to fade into her through the pores of her skin. She sat up, her eyes wide, a smile on her lips, and slowly pulled back the blanket from her bed and stood. Bishop coiled his muscles and raised his fur, spitting as she walked slowly across the floor toward the door.

"Silly Bishop," she said in a voice not truly her own. "I only want to play."

As she opened the door, the cat streaked past her into the darkness of the rest of the house. She seemed not to care as she walked slowly through the living room, pausing long enough to lay hands on every piece of furniture, every knick-knack, savoring each sensation of touch as though she'd not had physical sense for years. The air felt deliciously cool against her bare arms and legs. Even the chilly floor was a welcome sensation against her bare feet.

She walked slowly, almost lazily, through the living room door savoring each remembered sensation. She felt the texture of the pile carpet of the dining room on her toes and the smoothness of the cardboard boxes still patiently waiting to be unpacked. Her strength was fading fast with each step, each movement an expenditure of precious energy, but she was determined to enjoy every sensation until she could no longer continue.

She stopped in front of Shannon's door and stared, her face a mixture of fear and anger, seeming to see what was beyond the door. *She was in there.* She reached to push the door, and though it was cool to the touch, she recoiled as though burned. She could feel the heat radiating from inside, not physically, but in her thoughts, in her feelings. There was not enough energy left to fight. All in due time, she thought.

She smiled darkly as she turned and walked across the room to the door behind which Gabe and Trish slept. The door opened without a sound as she slid through the opening. Dear mother and father, she thought as she looked down on them. She moved silently around the bed to where her father snored softly.

"You'll be first," she said softly as she bent down to kiss his ear.

Gabe's eyes fluttered briefly open and struggled to focus on her.

"Honey? What's the matter?"

"You don't belong here," she replied mater-of-factly.

"Go back to bed," he mumbled as sleep reclaimed him. She smiled.

The last of her strength waning, she went back out, closing the door as silently as she'd opened it, and crossed the space between this room and hers. She made a wide circle around Shannon's door, never taking her eyes off the frame that seemed to glow white hot in her mind's eye. Back in her room, she climbed into bed and lay flat, her hands rested on her chest in perfect repose, and closed her eyes.

"Goodnight Celia," came Lizzy's sleepy whisper.

"Goodnight Lizzy," she replied to herself in that voice not her own.

CHAPTER 21

TOBY AND SARAH, CHILDREN AND DOUGHNUTS IN TOW, arrived early that morning just as Gabe was rolling out of bed. Trish was already awake, as was Shannon. He always felt it strange, no matter how early he got up on weekends, his wife and youngest child always seemed to get up earlier. Now, as he sat at the edge of his bed putting on a pair of tattered shorts, he wondered how she could function this early in the morning. His head still heavy with sleep, he walked to the bathroom and splashed cold water on his face and brushed his teeth.

Did he imagine, he wondered, that Lizzy had come into their room last night late? What was it she whispered to him? "You'll be first," or something like that. He shook his head and looked in the mirror. As he brushed his thick blond hair back, he half-decided he'd dreamed it. He pulled on his work-sneakers and a stained t-shirt and adjusted his favorite hat, a ball cap he'd gotten from Mardi Gras in 1999, then looked again in the mirror. While he doubted anyone would call him handsome in his present garb, he at least looked ready for work.

Pain ripped in jolts through his body as images flashed in his mind. He felt his knees buckle as, in the mirror, he could see Lizzy, a blade in hand, slashing him over and over, a smile of malicious glee on her lips.

He raised his hands in weak defense as the blade slashed through the air sending streams of gore splattering across the walls and mirrors. He watched in horror as the whizzing blade mutilated the flesh of his hands, and then as Lizzy raised the knife high above her head and howled, heralding the last strike.

He closed his eyes tight. When he opened his eyes, he was standing in front of the bathroom sink, as though nothing had happened. A quick check of his hands confirmed they were still intact. He stumbled backward and landed hard against the toilet. Rather than get up, he simply sat shaking, trying to regain his composure.

"Gabe?" There was pounding on the door. Trish's voice was full of worry. "Honey, are you alright?"

"Fine!" he yelped, less surprised by the sudden noise than by the strange visions. "I just fell. I'm fine."

"Hurry up," he heard his brother's voice say from farther away. "You're wasting daylight!"

Gabe cursed under his breath and forced himself to his feet. His knees were still shaky and his hands would not stop trembling, but he inhaled deeply and forced himself to put forth at least an outward image of calm, then he went to the kitchen, hoping no one would notice something wasn't right with him.

"'Morning, bro," called out Toby cheerfully as he drank his coffee and munched on a doughnut. "Ready for work?"

"Coffee first," he replied, scanning the room. "Where's Lizzy?"

"Still asleep," replied Trish. "I figured I'd just let her sleep until the work started. She won't be able to once you guys get the power tools going outside her window."

Gabe nodded as he filled up a proffered mug with steaming coffee. He couldn't shake the image of his daughter slashing at him with such animalistic glee. He took a doughnut from the box and dunked it in his coffee, savoring the sugary flavor mixed with the bitter elixir. He gestured with his mug toward the notebook on the table.

"Got lots to buy today," he said between mouthfuls.

Toby opened the notebook to the page marked with Gabe's pencil and let out a low whistle.

"Can you afford all this?"

Gabe shrugged. "I think so. Mom and Dad are giving me a month or two before I have to start making payments. Receipts go in the zipper bag there." He finished his doughnut and glanced at his watch. "C'mon," he said to his brother. "The hardware store is open by now."

They both took final drinks from their coffee mugs and marched out the door leaving Trish and Sarah with the toddlers. As they climbed into Toby's pickup truck, Gabe felt a measure of relief to be getting away from the house. Though his brother and he were always very close, he couldn't bring himself to relate what had really happened, or had not happened, in the bathroom. For now, he thought, it would be best if he said nothing.

A short and wordless drive later, they arrived at the hardware store. After spending nearly an hour finding the proper materials and tools, they had the clerk total the items. It didn't cost quite as much as they had thought, but it was still very expensive. Gabe called their parents with his cell phone, and, after the initial few moments of shock, they agreed. They paid at the register and, with the help of several clerks, loaded the materials and equipment into the bed of Toby's truck.

With the added weight and mass of wood and steel, Toby drove slowly through the back roads to the house, giving Gabe more unwelcome time to think. Every time he replayed the events in his mind, he could not help but draw conclusions to other happenings. The nightmares. The shaking. Trish's mysterious figure. The tar in Shannon's room. The voices. The footsteps.

"You're awfully quiet," Toby broke in. "What's the matter?"

"Nothing," replied Gabe curtly.

"Bullshit. You know you can't play that game with me. Now out with it."

Gabe took a deep breath. It was true his brother instinctively knew when something was bothering him. Even more annoying was that Toby would badger him about it until he knew what it was. Gabe decided not to fight it this time, but would only tell him what he was sure of.

"I'm not sure," he began. "Just weird stuff."

"Like what?"

"Trish and Lizzy aren't sleeping well. They haven't been since we moved in."

"Well, it is a new house."

"Yeah, I know." He sighed. "We've also been hearing things. I don't know what they are. Maybe the house settling, I guess. And no matter how I set the thermostat, Lizzy's room is always bitter cold and Shannon's room is always warm."

"Old houses are quirky," replied Toby.

"Yeah." He paused. "I've also been having weird dreams. So have the girls."

"Look," said Toby, giving him a reassuring smile. "You're all under a lot of stress. You're in a new house, you just declared bankruptcy, and Trish still doesn't have a job. You're entitled to a few bad dreams."

"I guess so," he said doubtfully.

"If I were going through what you're going through, I don't think I'd be able to handle it so well."

There came a long uncomfortable pause while Toby searched for the properly reassuring thing to say and Gabe debated whether or not to tell his brother the whole story. It was Toby who first broke the silence with a new subject.

"So what are we going to do today?" he enthused.

"Once we get this stuff home and unloaded, we need to sand each of these boards and prime them. Then we'll paint and seal them."

"And then?"

"Well," he continued, although he'd only given the next phase of his plan the most cursory of thoughts. "We have to pull the pillars off the front porch, repaint and seal them, pull off all the old boards, and replace them with the new ones."

"And just how do you intend we accomplish this feat?" Toby knew this was going to be a serious undertaking, because the pillars were set so the entire weight of the roof rested on them. Simply pulling them out would crack the spine of the house. Also, neither of them had seen beneath the rotten planks on the porch, save for the hole made by Gabe's leg. They had no way of knowing if there was more decay for them to deal with.

"I don't know," said Gabe irritably. "We'll just have to deal with that when we get to it."

The conversation for the rest of the ride home consisted of ideas bouncing back and forth about the best way to replace the floor of the porch without damaging the rest of the house. As they slid out of the truck, they decided it was best left unresolved for the time being and unloaded the bed of the truck into the garage.

After depositing the receipt and credit card in the zipper bag and tucking it away in its own drawer in the kitchen, Toby and Gabe went back to the garage. It took them a short while to sort through their purchases and unpack the belt-sanders and extension chords and other pieces of equipment, but once they had everything in its place, it was plain to see they would make relatively quick work of the job at hand.

Gabe glanced at his watch as his stomach began to gurgle with hunger. It was nearing lunch time and it seemed reasonable to start the actual work once they were done eating. He looked over toward his brother, who was making adjustments on his sander.

The way they had laid out the work space, each of them had two saw horses on either side of the garage, on which they each had placed a full sheet of eight-foot by five-foot, 3/4-inch thick plywood. Between the two areas, an extension chord ran with enough outlets for both sanders and a radio that sat between them. Gabe enjoyed working with his brother on any project and was happy to be doing so again.

"Lunch first," he barked, "then we start."

Toby grinned and nodded in agreement, and they headed back down the small narrow flight of stairs to the kitchen. True to form, Trish had already set out cold-cuts and other condiments for sandwiches. Shannon, Zachary and Vincent were already in their respective highchairs and were munching happily on cheese puffs while watching cartoons on the television. The only person conspicuous by her absence was Lizzy.

"Where's our oldest?" asked Gabe kissing his wife on the back of her head.

"Still asleep, I guess. She hasn't come out yet."

As if on cue, Lizzy trudged into the room, still in her nightgown, and plopped roughly into a chair.

"Well," said Toby brightly. "Good morning, sleepyhead."

Lizzy grunted in reply and stared at nothing in particular on the table. Gabe took a hard look at her face, which seemed paler to him than he was accustomed to. The bags beneath her eyes bothered him, and they were joined by a slight sallowness to her cheeks that bothered him even more. He could not help but remember the vision he'd had, of her stabbing over and over again with her face crazed and twisted. Now looking on her current condition, he could not help but feel the tiniest pangs of apprehension begin to kindle in his belly.

"Lizzy, honey," he began. He couldn't tell if it was the image of her with the knife or the way she looked now, or if he was just trying to be gentle, but the sound of his own voice came off more timid than he would have liked. "It's nearly noon. You need to get dressed and brush your hair and come eat something."

She slowly raised her head, and expression of complete exasperation on her face. Without a word, she threw herself up out of the chair and stomped off to her room. Gabe sheepishly looked around at the uncomfortably silent faces of Toby and Sarah.

"Adolescence," he said. "Fear it."

They ate their lunch in relatively good spirits, with conversation focusing on the many projects around the house and how wonderful it would be when they finally got it finished. Midway through the meal Lizzy returned, dressed in jean shorts and a t-shirt. She plopped down on the couch and brushed her tangled hair as she absently stared at the television screen.

"Come get something to eat, honey," said Gabe lightly.

"Not hungry," came the far away reply.

"That's not a request," he said with forced kindness as he got up and cleared away his space. "You need to eat." He pretended not to notice the venomous look she gave him as he made his way for the garage, but he could feel it as if it were screws of ice burrowing into his neck.

"I'll be out in a minute!" Toby called after him as the door closed. Gabe heard his brother, but didn't respond. He could come up when he finished eating. Gabe felt angry and embarrassed by the actions of his oldest daughter. It was bad enough that she'd been disrespectful and rude, but in front of guests? Especially her uncle. That sort of behavior was intolerable.

He pulled a fresh pack of cigarettes from his pocket and, extracting one, threw the pack on his workspace. He crossed to the bench as he lit the butt and inhaled deeply. He pulled the old iron ashtray off the counter and went back to the waiting plank. He blew out forcefully through his nose, placing the ashtray on an overturned bucket beside his chair.

She sleeps till noon, then gets up and acts like she needs a nap, he glowered. What the hell was that all about? He clicked on the sander and began rhythmically coursing across the board, all the while fuming and chewing on the end of his cigarette.

Strange things all around him, he thought. Trish and her imagination, Lizzy getting snippier and closer to teen-aged years by the second, and now he was beginning to show signs of wear. He shut off the sander for a moment and took a deep breath. Whatever he'd imagined in the bathroom had affected him more than he'd realized. If only he knew what it had been, or if it would happen again. Maybe the house was haunted.

"You okay?"

He looked up to see Toby standing in the doorway, a look of amused concern on his face. Though, in Gabe's mind, concern and amusement were mutually exclusive terms, Toby seemed to be able to combine them masterfully.

"Yeah," he replied. "It's just frustrating."

"You can't let kids get to you like that," he said. "She's perfectly normal."

"I'm going to remind you of that in a few years when Zach hits this age." He paused for a moment. "So what happened after I left the room?"

Toby sauntered over to his work area and sat down. "She grumbled a bit, but sat down and ate a sandwich. She really is a good kid, y'know. She pretty much does what you tell her to."

"I know," he said. It was true. For all of her complaining and sullen attitudes, she did what was asked of her and he knew he could depend on her to make good decisions. It was that very thought that seemed to make her current attitude seem so infuriating. It just wasn't like her. Lizzy was normally a very sweet child, whose disposition was rarely sour and did, for the most part, what she was told. She always seemed to be bright, upbeat and energetic. But now, here, she was sullen, always tired, always irritable.

He clicked on his sander and went back to work. Toby, seeing that the conversation was temporarily on hiatus, did the same. It took them several hours to finish sanding the boards to their satisfaction. After it was smooth enough, they primed it and left it to dry over night. Rome was not built in one day, and neither would be this porch.

Next they went around to the front of the house, took measurements from top to bottom of each pillar, taking special notice of which were in the most dire need of repair. After a goodly amount of time, when the primer was dry enough that the boards could be moved, they helped each other shift the sanded planks off the sawhorses and rough ones on. With each of them working on a separate plank at once, they were able to get all six planks sanded and primed in a single day.

They had stood the sheets of plywood upright, leaning only the slightest bit against the walls, giving the garage the look of an entirely different room. When they were finished, they went back down the small flight of stairs to the kitchen. Gabe closed the heavy outside door to the garage as he went inside. Tomorrow, he said to himself, he would try to figure out with some finality how he was going to pull out the columns and replace the floor.

CHAPTER 22

TRISH AWOKE TO THE SOUND OF DISTANT YELLING. She reached to shake her husband, only to find him missing. She listened intently for a moment, realizing that it was Gabe who was throwing some sort of tantrum. She pulled on her terrycloth robe and followed the voice through the kitchen to the garage. As she crept up the stairs she could hear him cursing loudly and banging tools around. She slid the door open and found him standing barefoot, wearing only a pair of dirty shorts, taking the belt off one of the sanders.

"Honey?" she asked.

He whirled around, surprised by the sudden intrusion.

"What?!" Then, seeing the identity of the interloper, his expression softened to one less of manic rage, but more of frustration. "I'm sorry. Did I wake you?"

"What are you doing out here?" she asked as she crossed the threshold of the garage.

"I woke up," he said flatly. "I came out here to smoke, and look at what I found when I did."

She followed his outstretched hand with her eyes until she saw the cause of his anger. On each of the boards they had worked on so arduously for the day were long scratches and gouges. It was as though some great beast with claws of steel had marked its territory against the white primed surfaces. At the bottom corner of the foremost board was what appeared to be a handprint, the size of a child's, in the paint.

"What happened?"

"Well it seems pretty obvious to me," he growled. "I guess Lizzy decided she needed attention. Now I've got to start over on all of this."

Trish was immediately defensive at the accusation of Lizzy.

"What makes you think it was her?" she demanded.

Gabe turned to face her with a look of incredulity.

"Did you do it?" he almost shouted.

"Of course not!"

"Well I sure didn't do it, and I doubt Shannon could have done it, so that leaves one person with a hand this size," he said, growing angrier as he approached the small hand print to illustrate his point.

"But why would she...?"

"I don't know," he cut her off. "Why don't you go ask her?"

"Keep your voice down," she hissed. "It's nearly four in the morning!"

"I don't care!" he bellowed, and then caught himself. "I'm sorry," he said. "I'm just a little angry right now."

"I understand," she said, putting her arm around his shoulders. "And I agree that whoever did this needs to be punished. But I'm not so quick to accuse Lizzy." She took his hand and pulled him toward the stairs. "Come back to bed. It's late and it's not like you could do anything about it now anyway. We'll ask her about it in the morning."

As they crossed into the kitchen they noticed Bishop moving close to the ground and peering behind him into the older part of the house, his tail fluffed out in a sign of fear. Trish was reaching to pick up the frightened feline when at once they both heard it. Giggling. The quiet laughter of a little girl who watched a prank unfold while she hid. Trish and Gabe looked at each other with wide eyes.

"Lizzy..." muttered Gabe under his breath as he made his way quickly in the direction of the sound. Trish followed closely behind, fearful, not only that in his present state of mind her husband would do something rash, but also at the churning in her stomach that told her he was wrong.

Through the darkness of the house they could hear the sounds of bare running feet against the living room floor accompanied by the same laughter that seemed impossible to stifle. As they stepped across the threshold of the kitchen they were both engulfed in bitter cold. Trish could feel herself panic, as though she'd had this feeling before, but for some reason could not remember. Instinctively she latched on to Gabe's arm.

"Wait," she said, her voice filled with panic.

"What?" he hissed, turning on her. The look of rage in his eyes only increased her sense of danger.

"Something's not right here," she pleaded. She could not find the words to tell him. They were in danger, she knew, but from what? How could she make him understand when she couldn't articulate her own feeling?

Gabe looked as though he was about to say something when they heard it again. The laughter was clearer now, more distinct, closer. The looked in its direction and saw its source, or rather did not see it. Silhouetted against the moonlit windows was the shape of a little girl in a long nightgown.

Gabe could feel the hairs on the nape of his neck prickle.

"Lizzy?" he asked quietly.

"No," said Trish, her voice barely more than a whisper. "Not Lizzy." Fear welled up inside her as she immediately remembered the figure in the bathroom. Though she could not make out features either time, she was sure it was the same.

The figure darted in the direction of Lizzy's room, sending Gabe and Trish hurtling after it, a gnawing dread taking over their sensibilities. All thoughts of logical explanations or paranormal activity were erased by the simple instinctive knowledge that something was in the house and it was headed for their child.

They raced to the door of Lizzy's room and tried the knob. Though the knob gave and turned, the door still would not open. From behind the door they could hear the giggling voice taunting them. As they leaned into the door to try to force it open, Gabe could hear a distinctly different sound, like fingernails scraping down the inside of the door.

He threw his body against the door again. Trish could see wildly moving shadows in the empty flue above the door and let out a panic-stricken cry of frustration as she continued to pound against the door with her husband. The bitter cold made each strike against the wooden door agony against their bodies, but they either did not notice or did not care.

The door flew open, sending them temporarily sprawling into Lizzy's room. Gabe was the first to his feet and looked wildly about the room, searching for any sign of the intruder. Trish righted her self with more caution, noticing the biting cold that seemed intent on stopping them was retreating somewhat. She also noticed that Lizzy had slept through the entire event and was even now snoring softly with drool on her pillow.

Did they imagine it? Could it have been a trick of light and shadow? Gabe began to doubt what they had seen when he heard it again, this time behind him. He spun quickly to see the dark silhouette standing no more than five feet from him. Despite its close proximity, he could still see no trace of features, lines separating clothing from flesh, hair from face. It was as though a shadow had torn itself from the wall and now was confronting him with an icy air around it.

Without warning, it darted back through the house, and although he did not know why or how, Gabe knew where it was going.

"Shannon."

He ran to the room where his angelic toddler slept, leaving Trish desperately trying to wake Lizzy from a sleep that more resembled a coma. He reached the door and grabbed the knob, flinching momentarily at the burning pain that jolted through his hand. The handle of the door was searingly hot, almost immediately raising blisters on the palm and fingers of his hand.

Ignoring the pain, he heaved with all of his weight against the door, throwing it open. The room was hot enough to be stifling. Sweat poured from his forehead and off his back as he searched the room feverishly, but he knew what he would not find. Somehow, before he'd even gotten to the door, he knew. Shannon was not in her room.

"No!" he screamed, an animalistic cry more than words, as he leaped toward her bed, tearing the blankets off as if she could be hiding amongst them. "Shannon!" he howled as he continued his search, overturning her bed and pulling boxes this way and that. In the end, it was useless. Shannon was simply not in the room.

He ran back to where his wife and oldest daughter, who was now awake and groggy, sat on the bed, both their eyes wide in fear.

"Shannon's gone!"

"What do you mean, 'gone?'"

"She's not in her room! I went after that... that... thing, and she's gone!" The fear had overtaken him. He was babbling, but the meaning of his words was still clear as the panic that held him leaped like wildfire into Trish's soul. Lizzy snapped out of her half-waked state into full sobriety at the mention of her sister's name and jumped to the floor.

Gabe ran from the room and began looking around the house calling for Shannon. Trish, with Lizzy firmly by the hand, did the same in any room Gabe was not presently in. As they were about to pass Shannon's room, Trish stopped abruptly, nearly pulling her daughter down in the process.

"Come on!" cried Lizzy as she tugged with all of her might at her mother's arm, but she would not budge an inch.

"She's in there," she said so quietly that Lizzy was unsure if she had heard her.

"I already looked in there," growled Gabe as he passed by, continuing his furtive search.

Trish raised her hand to the door, which opened with little effort. She walked somnambulistically through the door into the wet heat of the room, pulling her daughter behind her.

"Mom," Lizzy whined. "Let go of me. It's too hot in here."

"Hush child," barked her mother, making Lizzy jump. Her mother had never spoken to her like that, nor had she ever simply referred to her as "child."

As they slowly walked through the room, Lizzy began to feel a swell of panic, as though the walls of the room were closing in around her, pressing down against her mind, trying to drive her back out into the house, but still her mother continued deeper into the room until she got to the bathroom door.

"In here," she said quietly. She pushed the door open and walked in, to the other door on the adjoining wall. Beyond that door was the large workroom that had been added later to the house. Lizzy was beginning to feel sick from the room pressing down upon her. It was enough to make her sob quietly as her mother's grip tightened around her wrist.

"Mom," she cried. "You're hurting me."

Trish ignored her and opened the door to the workroom. As she stepped through the doorway, she collapsed, as did Lizzy, on the cool tile floor. The looked around in the darkness, trying to locate each other, navigating by touch. Trish got to her feet and felt along the wall for the lightswitch. She clicked it on and almost immediately let out a cry of relief and joy. There, sitting in the center of the room amid all the boxes and bric-a-brac was Shannon, bottle in hand, playing happily with the strange little burlap doll. She smiled when she saw her mother.

"Mommy!" She got up grinning and ran to Trish who cradled her in her arms, tear rolling down her cheeks. "Sissy!" she smiled and wrapped her free arm around her sister's neck, hugging them both tightly.

"Gabe!" she called. "I found her!"

Almost instantly, he appeared in the doorway, his face a mask of relief and disbelief. On sight of her father, Shannon released Trish and Lizzy. "Daddy!" she cried, pushing herself upright and running to Gabe, who scooped her up and kissed her tiny face. Tears of happiness streamed down his face as she snuggled her face into his neck.

"Wadda madder?" she asked.

"Daddy couldn't find you," he said smiling. "How'd you get in here?"

"Lady," she said as she snuggled back against him.

Gabe threw a concerned look at Trish and Lizzy. My God, he thought, what's happening to us?

CHAPTER 23

With no rent to pay, the matter was fairly simple. Simply put off paying a few of the mounting pile of bills, the creditors be hanged. After quickly gathering a few items of clothing, they had found a hotel with 24-hour check in service and, after a few minutes discussion about whether or not the cat could stay with them in their room, booked a room with two full beds.

As his wife and children slept peacefully for the first time in a while, Gabe stood outside, the door cracked open just a bit, smoking and trying to make sense of what had happened. His hands still shook with the fear that comes with having one's beliefs crumble before his eyes. Although fatigue wracked his body, his mind still raced and he knew he would be unable to sleep. Rather than keep his family from what seemed to be the first undisturbed sleep since they'd moved in, he sat and pondered on the thin walkway outside their room.

Under any normal circumstance, he would pack up his children and leave the house, damn the real estate agency, to find some place less dangerous. It would be easy to leave, forget their belongings and start over somewhere else. But that was not an option for them. They had no where else to go.

Depression began to sink in as, in his mind, he replayed every event that had lead to their financial ruin. By pure luck and coincidence, he'd gotten a job with the university before he'd graduated, telling himself that he could still finish his degree. Seven years later, he finally accomplished that goal, but what if, he thought, he'd just toughed out another few semesters instead of taking the job? Inside, he told himself that what seemed like a good idea at the time actually kept him from getting a better paying job, and had he continued, they would not be in this predicament.

He had, against his better judgment, agreed to purchase the house in neighboring South Austin because his wife worked in the park where the home was to be located, only for her to be fired by the self-serving bastard who had employed her. As a direct result of her dismissal, the house payment could no longer be made and the lease on the land was terminated.

It was a crushing blow to Trish, who prided herself on her work ethic. Now, discouraged and doubting her own self-worth, she was not ready to look for another job. It was also when they found out about the impending arrival of Shannon.

By the time they had finally landed in the old house in San Marcos, bills had piled up, creditors were calling daily, and they'd had to file bankruptcy, making getting an apartment next to impossible, not that they could afford one on Gabe's limited salary alone.

It was his meager paycheck that made Gabe feel, somehow, he was to blame for the entire mess. In his mind, he had failed to provide for his family. He appreciated his wife's willingness to work, but it grieved him that she had to work in order for them to afford food. If only he'd been smarter. If only he'd finished his degree and gotten a better job. If only he'd listened to his instinct about the house. If only…

It hurt him when his children asked him to buy them new toys, and always came the same limping reply of not having enough money. He hated that his wife often wore threadbare clothing because they had to pay bills. And now his family was in jeopardy, and this too was his fault. The realization made him feel less of a man.

The love of his family often was the only thing that kept him from complete despair. Lizzy's shining smile as she told him it was alright. She'd written a poem and shared it with her class in fourth grade about her father, and how she wished she could buy him a new car because he could not afford one on his own. The admission to her classmates made him weep.

It seemed to him now, they too would know what a failure he was. Trish did not complain often about the lack of money, and would hold him and tell him he was wonderful, but inside his heart he felt incomplete. He felt she deserved more than a loser like him, and though her words were meant to encourage, all they did was deepen the chasm his depression.

Shannon had proven to be the one bright moment of that time. When she was born, he was there and wept openly as he cradled her naked body in his arms. He'd always wished he could have been there when Lizzy was born, but he loved her as though she were his own. Shannon, on the other hand, was his own. His first.

But now...

He sank down to the floor as he lit another cigarette. My God, he thought, where did I go wrong? The house had seemed like such a good idea at the time. His mother and father wanted to be closer to their grandchildren when they retired, and saw the house as reassurance that wherever they moved, he would be a permanent resident. It was, in no small part, his doing that they'd spent their retirement money on this house which now threatened them.

Logic dictated they should simply get out of the house. His family was in danger, so the smart thing to do would be to get them out of danger. But then what? Where would they go? All he'd ever wanted was to provide a home for his family. He wanted to live up to his father's example of a provider. And now he was being driven from his chance to do that by some phantom that invaded their dreams and possessed his children.

He felt a kindling of anger smoldering within him. My children, he thought. Of the things well known about Gabe, he readily admitted to being over-protective. His children were more precious to him than his own life. For something, anything, to be threatening his children was a sin he could not bear. The small ember of anger caught and rage blazed through his soul. He would not just roll over and accept the loss. This time, he decided, he was going to fight.

Noiselessly, he slipped back into the hotel room where his wife and children lay sleeping. Shannon clutched the strange little burlap doll in one hand tightly and her bottle in the other as she giggled softly in her sleep. Lizzy looked as if she were not dreaming at all, only letting her body finally heal after the long ordeal that she'd gone through. Trish slept deeply and had not moved since she'd first lay down well over an hour ago.

He kissed each of them softly, so as not to wake them, and hastily scribbled a note in the hotel-provided stationary. He placed the note on top of the television and glanced at his watch. It was just after 5 a.m. on Sunday. He took one last look at his family as he closed the door behind himself.

"Don't worry," he said at a whisper. "Daddy's going to make you proud. Watch over them Bishop," he said to the fluffy cat who sat sentinel-like at Lizzy's feet.

CHAPTER 24

As he sped through the empty streets, his thoughts raced and his fury intensified. By the time he arrived at the house, he wanted nothing more than to confront the specter of the house, to somehow drive it out by sheer will alone. For once in his life, he was going to do something right and claim the house for his family.

As he pulled into the driveway, his stomach knotted as fear began to creep into his mind. Just what the hell did he think he was doing? He knew nothing about what he was facing. Up until a few short hours ago, he didn't believe in ghosts, and now that he did he wished he knew more about them.

He slid out onto the shell driveway and walked slowly toward the house. He couldn't be sure if it was the nagging fear and self-doubt that made it seem so, but the shadows around the house seemed to thicken behind him, taking him in and obscuring the passage out to freedom.

He took several deep breaths to try to quell the fear that threatened to overtake him and make him run back up the stone stairs to his car where he would drive away, never to see the house again.

If he left now, he told himself, he'd never return. He either went in to confront his problem, or he ran and lived as a coward. He steeled his courage and opened the door.

The house was eerily quiet. Not even the hiss of the air conditioner, nor the hum of the refrigerator, could be heard. It was cold enough he could see his breath in front of him. He scanned the room for any sign of movement, any trace of life, but there was none. Only the shadows and the cold stared back at him from the walls.

He took several steps into the kitchen, the fear inside him prickling his skin and making his every footfall seem like thunder. The shadows were grotesque and exaggerated on the walls, only increasing his own paranoia. As he approached the doorway into the older section of the house, he took one more deep breath, then, eyes wide, he stepped across the threshold into palpable darkness that seemed to want to smother him.

Now what? He'd made it inside without so much as a rattling plate. His nerves were raw with the anticipation of the confrontation to come.

"Alright," he said aloud. "You wanted my attention? You got it."

Almost immediately, he heard whispers. The same whispers with a thousand voices that they'd heard over the monitor that first night. The whispers that sounded like locust wings with words in them. They buzzed hotly in his ears, although he couldn't make out the words they were saying. He turned around as though looking for the source, although he knew he'd never find it.

"I can't understand you!" he yelled. "And I don't give a damn! Leave my family alone!"

A blast of icy air ripped through the hallway and stabbed at him, making his knees buckle. He hit the floor hard, the pain intensified by the cold. He could taste blood in his mouth amid the frozen spit that made it difficult to breathe. His muscles began to stiffen as the cold worked its way into them.

"Get out of my house!" he croaked as loudly as he could, but in the howl of the wind it sounded shallow even to his own ears. His cry was heard, he realized, as another burst of icy air hit him like a hammer, knocking him backward against a wall, cracking the plaster.

My house he heard the whispers say in his mind. All around him he could see the shadows twist and congeal into one single mass that formed in the eye of the windstorm. It strengthened from translucence into deeply solid until at last he could make out the shape of the girl he'd seen earlier that night. Now, in his current situation, the image of the little girl was as terrifying a sight as he'd ever seen.

"What do you want from us?" he screamed against the wind.

I want to play with them, the whispers became stronger voices inside his head, growing in volume until they drowned out everything save the howling of the wind. *You*, it said, *don't belong here.*

As the words grew in intensity, he could feel his head begin to throb, as though some force was squeezing him from the waist, the pressure building in his head.

"They're my family!" he roared despite the pain.

We don't need you. You don't belong here.

With that proclamation, the howling in his ears grew to fever pitch, and the pressure in his skull increased such that he felt his head would surely burst. The shadow figure drifted toward him, the dark and wispy limbs reaching out to take him in. He closed his eyes in fear, sorrow welling up within him as he realized he had failed, and now would leave his family alone.

His body tensed as he felt the cold closing in on him, lifting him from the ground, pinning him to the wall, crushing the air from his lungs. His only thought was that he hoped his family was not as stupid as he, and they would get away from the house. He was feeling the darkness enshroud his mind and invade his body as unconsciousness claimed him.

In the dimmest corner of his vision, he saw a flicker of light, a candle-sized flame, appear in the darkness. It moved toward him, growing stronger with every inch until the radiating warmth began to drive the cold from his body. The pain of the cold pulling itself from down his throat was excruciating, and he fell to the floor retching, his head still throbbing against whatever pressure had been exerted on him. He could not help but to turn his head to see what had driven the icy fingers away from him.

A column of flame, he guessed six feet wide and as tall as the vaulted ceilings, spun before him, its tongues spitting in all directions.

Get out, he heard a new voice, or choir of voices like bells, say inside his head.

"Who... who are..." he stammered.

Get out, it said louder.

"But... But this is..."

GET OUT!

The final shout hit him with such force that he was sent reeling through the doorway on his belly. He scrambled to the back door with the burning edict still echoing in his mind. He threw himself out the door and landed hard on the terra-cotta patio. There he lay, for how long he could not determine, until he'd mustered the strength to stand and painfully move up the stone steps to his car.

Once inside, with the doors firmly secured, he pulled the wrinkled pack of cigarettes from his pocket and extracted one. He found the lighter he kept in the car and flicked the flame to life. As he inhaled the smoke deeply, he continued to stare at the flame that danced on top of the lighter. Although he knew it to be memory, he still heard the words clearly enough to shudder at their sound.

His hands shook so badly it took him a few minutes to get his keys in the ignition, and although he was not certainhe was steady enough to drive, he knew he did not want to stay at the house. It had beaten him, he knew. If not for the other - what could he call it? - thing, he'd surely be dead. He jammed the car into gear and drove slowly off through the streets in time to see the sunrise.

CHAPTER 25

TRISH AWOKE WITH A START with the instinctive knowledge something in her world was not right. A voice in her head and a clutching in her stomach told her that her husband had done something well meaning, but foolish. She got up and found the note he left for her on the television, confirming her fears: He had gone back to the house.

Now, without the slightest idea of when, or even if, he would return, she stood on the thin walkway outside their hotel room smoking, anxiety gripping her from the inside. The children still slept peacefully, watched over by Bishop, who seemed intent on not leaving his young mistresses for any reason. It was just as well, she decided as she scratched his head and went outside, praying that soon she would see the headlights of her husband's car pull in to the parking lot.

She didn't have to wait long. As the sun began its ascent, their little white SUV pulled slowly into a parking space. The joy she felt at seeing the car was quickly replaced by horror as he fairly fell out of it, his face bloody and his movements limping.

She raced down the stairs to him as he clung to the hood of the car. It was obvious whatever he'd set out to do, he'd been unsuccessful. She reached him and looped his arm around her shoulders, praying she had the strength to help him up the stairs.

"Hi honey," he said weakly.

"Jesus, Gabe," she said, her voice choked with tears. "What did you do?"

"I failed again," he said, his voice full of sorrow and pain. "I tried to do the right thing, but I failed again."

She held him close as they went up the stairs.

"It's alright," she lied. "I've got you now." He'd live, she realized, which allowed her fear to give way to anger. What was he thinking, going to the house alone like that? She knew he blamed himself for all of their problems, but it was ridiculous. It wasn't his fault, so why did he feel compelled to put his body and life in jeopardy to pull them out of a bad situation?

Of course, that quality was one of the things she loved about him. He was very quick to take responsibility for any given situation and to try to rectify it. But this time, from the looks of him, she almost lost him for good, and then where would she be? Her family meant everything to her, and Gabe was the person who had given her hope many years ago. He was always there for her, and she couldn't believe how close she had come to losing him.

They went into the room as quietly as they could and she sat him down on the bed. His body was limp from exhaustion as she peeled off his t-shirt and laid him gently down on the pillow. She pulled gently at his shoes and placed them by the nightstand then went to the bathroom, wet a washcloth, and returned to wipe the crusted blood from his face.

It hurt her greatly when she ran the cold cloth over his mouth to see his lips split and swelling. When she was done, his fatigue was so great that he lay down and fell into a deep sleep. Trish curled up behind him, although she knew she could not find sleep herself, and held him until he regained consciousness several hours later.

CHAPTER 26

PROFESSOR DONALD THORNDYKE SAT in his dimly lit office at his computer, searching for records via the internet. There was something clearly wrong in that house in which his friend resided, but getting the poor boy to open up and just believe there are more things unseen than seen in this world was, to say the least, difficult. He'd been researching off and on throughout the weekend, but more as a passing interest.

Today, however, when he saw Gabe's office door still locked and the department secretary said he had called in sick, he feared the worst. Gabe had never, in the seven years he'd known him, called in sick. He'd dragged himself in looking like death warmed over, but he'd never called in sick. He called up his list of bookmarked pages where he could find records of births and deaths, obituaries and news archives and set to work in earnest trying to solve the riddle that no one had asked of him: What was in that house?

He'd been working steadily for nearly two hours when a tired haggard figure appeared in his doorway. The boy looked as though he'd been in a prize fight and came out on the losing end of it. The serious look on his face kept Don from asking flippantly what happened. Instead, he simply waited for the gaunt and beaten figure to speak. When he did speak, it was only two words.

"I believe," said Gabe.

And they were off in a mad dash, classes be damned.

CHAPTER 27

In the hotel room, Lizzy sat at the edge of her bed alongside her mother, who had Shannon in her lap. Gabe sat directly across from them on the other bed, with Thorndyke taking a chair from the nearby desk. He had out a small spiral-bound notebook into which he was quickly jotting notes. Don insisted the children stay, reminding Gabe that they were a part of what was happening too.

"But Shannon doesn't even understand what's going on here," retorted Trish.

Don's eyes met Shannon's for a long gaze. "I think this little angel understands what's going on better than you or I, don't you sweetheart?"

As if in answer, Shannon giggled and hid her face playfully.

"Now," he said with authority. "Tell me exactly what happened."

"Where do we begin?" asked Trish.

"At the beginning," he replied. "Tell me everything that happened from the time you first walked through the door to the time you showed up at my office."

The story began to unfold, each taking their turn with their own sights and versions of the haunting. They told him of the running footsteps, the violent shaking, the whispered voices that came in the night, the attic, the dreams no one could seem to remember, and so on until they had finally spun the entire tale.

"And what on earth," he said turning a cocked eyebrow toward Gabe, "led you to think going back there with a good mad on would accomplish anything?"

"I was upset," said Gabe sheepishly. "I didn't know what else to do. I was tired of feeling worthless and helpless." Trish hugged him tight.

"You're damned lucky it didn't kill you," said Don flatly. "Ghosts, or more specifically in your case, a presence, are cyclical. They only manifest themselves when there is energy present. They expend energy until there is no more, then they lay dormant until they can rebuild it. That's why these things always start small. When you walked in there looking to pick a fight, you gave it enough energy to feed off of to kill you."

"So it's a poltergeist," said Gabe, trying to catch up with years of disbelieving ignorance.

"No," said Don thoughtfully. "A poltergeist is actually undirected energy, and not usually a ghost at all. A presence, such as the one you have, shows intelligence and awareness."

"I didn't know," he said quietly.

"Your actions are commendable," said Thorndyke, softening a bit. "It's the rare man nowadays who will put himself in harms way to defend his family. But next time, find out what you're dealing with before you go off half-cocked."

"I thought ghosts couldn't hurt people," chimed in Lizzy, who had been strangely silent throughout the entire meeting. "That's what my books said. 'Ghosts are merely displaced spirits with unfinished business, but are relatively harmless.'"

The three adults gaped at her as though she'd just sprouted another head. She became immediately self-conscious and dropped her eyes to the floor.

Don squatted down in front of her.

"What a bright little girl," he beamed. "Where did you learn about such things?"

"I have books," she said. "I read as much about this stuff as I can. But my books were wrong. Ghosts can hurt people." She began to get angry. "Look what it did to my daddy!" Great angry tears rolled down her cheeks as she looked again on the swollen eyes and puffy nose of her father, who had earlier returned with much of his blood dripping from cuts and abrasions inflicted by apparition.

"Your books didn't lie," he said sweetly, patting her knee. "They just didn't tell you the whole story. You see, there are many different types of 'ghosts.' Most of them can't hurt you, nor do they want to. But some, some who died violently, or perhaps were unkind in life, or who are just plain angry for whatever reason, they can be most dangerous." He patted her shoulder. "When this whole ordeal is over, if you're still interested, you can read some of my books. I could always use a research assistant. Especially one so capable and intelligent." Lizzy beamed.

"Now," he said. "Are you quite sure you told me everything? What stopped the thing from killing you?" he asked Gabe.

"Well, there was another in the house. This one was... I don't know how to describe it. It was like this thing was the polar opposite of the other one. Where one was cold, this one was a column of fire..."

"Fire?" asked Don with intrigue in his voice. "Do you remember what Doris, at the historical society, told you about your house?"

"Yeah."

"I think the entities trapped in the house are poor little Celia Tinsley and her mother, Hester."

"It is," said Lizzy quietly. Again, the three adults gaped at her. "At least, Celia is."

"How do you know that, honey?" asked Gabe.

"She told me," replied Lizzy. "She's my friend."

"Why didn't you tell us about her before?" asked Trish with urgency. "When everything was happening, when we were all so frightened, why didn't you tell us?"

"I thought if I told you the house was haunted, you'd want to leave. And I thought you'd blame all the bad stuff on Celia. But I knew it couldn't be her. I knew it had to be someone else. She couldn't do that kind of stuff. She told me we had to keep it a secret that she was here, because if you knew about her, you'd make us move again. Besides, you wouldn't have believed me."

Don considered for a moment, then stood abruptly. "Thank you Lizzy. Would you mind watching your sister for a moment while I talk to your parents outside?"

She nodded dejectedly, but said nothing as the three adults went to the walkway outside their hotel room. She turned the television on to cartoons and moved closer to the door to try to catch bits of the conversation outside.

"She's remarkable," said Don, lighting his pipe.

"We like to think so," said Gabe as he lit his wife's cigarette then his own.

"You don't understand," he replied. "I mean she is truly remarkable in the sense that she has no idea the untapped power inside her. Probably because of her age. Do you know how rare it is for a person to be able to actually talk to a ghost?" They shook their heads. "Your daughter has all the makings for a top-notch medium. Now tell me, has she been behaving erratically?"

"Well, she is an adolescent girl," said Trish with a half smile.

"I mean has she seemed unusually edgy? Does she sleep alot, or have fitful sleep? Or does she have nightmares or sleepwalk?"

"Well, yes," said Gabe. "On all three counts."

"I fear your daughter may have more into this than she knows. I think she's in the early stages of possession."

Gabe and Trish stood staring in horror at the old professor.

"Let me explain. This being that has befriended Lizzy seems to want no one to know about it. You said yourself her room was often very cold following a disturbance. And, you also said, she has begun sleepwalking and she looks tired and pale since you've been in the house. However, after one night away from the house, she looks well rested and healthy. Doesn't any of that strike you as odd?"

They said nothing, only looked fearfully to each other and back to the old professor.

"I think," he was trying to be gentle, but, given the subject matter, it was impossible. "I think this being is trying to gain her trust so it can invade her body and essentially live again."

"What can we do?" asked Trish quietly as tears welled in her eyes.

"I would like to try an experiment," he said. "Often times, it seems ghosts leave an imprint in the minds of their hosts. I would like to try to learn more about this being through hypnosis."

"You've gotta be kidding me!" scoffed Gabe. "Hypnosis!?"

"Remember, you're the one who didn't believe in ghosts until last night. I assure you it's perfectly safe. And if I'm right," he said, eyes twinkling, "then we may find out why the house is haunted and what this other is. We might even find out how to rid the house of this presence."

Gabe considered for a moment. He was hesitant to put his child in harm's way. If Don was correct, it would be worth knowing what this creature was and how to get rid of it. If he was incorrect, he could cause irreparable damage. But if it truly were harmless, as Don said, he had no worry. He turned to Trish.

"Why don't you take Shannon for a drive," he said. "Get us some dinner maybe." He hated to send her away, but Shannon would disrupt the session, he knew, and there was no way he was letting Lizzy out of his sight. Trish, thankfully, understood and went to gather up Shannon and a diaper bag. He kissed her goodbye and watched as the car pulled out of the parking lot, then turned a steely eye on his friend.

"I'm trusting you," he said, his voice full of warning.

CHAPTER 28

"Lizzy," said Don softly. "Can you hear me?"

"Yes," she replied sleepily.

She was in a deep trance, able to hear only the professor's voice. Gabe felt uncomfortable in the darkened room with his daughter on the bed and the old man speaking directly into her ear. He wanted to be doing something, anything. Anything but this.

"Lizzy," he said again. "Tell me about Celia."

"She's a little girl who died in our house," she said dreamily. "She's so sad and lonely. She's my friend."

"Does she show you things?"

"Yes."

"What kinds of things does she show you?"

"I can't remember."

"Lizzy, we're going to go deeper into sleep now," he said gently. "I want you to picture a long stairwell. You are at the top of it. I'm going to count backward from twenty. You will begin to walk slowly down that flight of stairs. Is that alright?"

"Ceilia wouldn't like it."

"Ceilia is not here now," reminded Don. "It will be alright. Twenty. You can feel yourself taking the steps down the stairwell. Nineteen.

Eighteen."

Gabe watched as Lizzy's hands tightened around the comforter on the bed. Her brow wrinkled. "What's the matter with her?" he blurted.

Don looked on her face and hands and ceased counting.

"Lizzy?" he asked. "What's the matter?"

"I'm afraid," she replied. Her voice sounded oddly detached to Gabe.

"There is no need to be afraid," soothed Don. "What do you see?"

"Fire," she said, the word settling like a stone in Gabe's stomach.

"Lizzy," he said immediately. "The stairway is gone. The fire is gone. You no longer are in the fire." Her hands relaxed. "We're going to go back, but now you will see things only as an observer. Nothing you see can hurt you. Do you understand?"

"Yes," she said.

"Now, you're standing at the top of the stairs again. At the bottom of the stairs you can see a door. Can you see the door?"

"Yes."

"We're going to count backward from five," he said. "When we reach one, you will open the door. Five, four, three, two, one. What do you see Lizzy?"

"I see a man in a long black coat," she said, her voice still dream like.

"Tell me about the man."

"He has a thick moustache. Celia calls him Daddy."

"What is he doing?"

"He's lying in a box. There are coins over his eyes. His clothes are pulled up tight around him. Celia has to sit with him. It's her fault that he's in the box."

Gabe felt a sob land like a fist in his throat. No wonder the child was sad. No wonder her soul could not rest. Her crazy mother blamed her for the death of her husband.

"She shows me his face, how it changes. He looks like my daddy now." She looked as though she was about to say something else, but stopped.

"What else does she show you?"

"She shows me her daddy's razor." Her voice began to quicken as panic and fear began to creep again into her mind. "She tells me my daddy shouldn't be here. She tells me he doesn't belong." She was becoming hysterical. Gabe looked to Don, who stared unblinking at the little girl who grew more agitated by the moment. "She tells me where she hid the razor. She tells me I have to kill my daddy!" She sat bolt upright and began to scream hysterically.

"Daddy! Daddy!"

Gabe rushed to her side, only to be held back by Don, who quickly covered her eyes with his hand.

"Sleep," he said simply, and Lizzy's body went limp. Don gently settled her back onto the pillow.

"What the hell was that!?" cried Gabe, louder than he intended. "What are you doing to my daughter!?"

"Be quiet," commanded Don in a quiet but forceful voice. Gabe sat stunned on the bed next to him. "We're almost done, then I promise you she'll be none the worse for wear."

"Lizzy," he began again. "You've stepped back through the door and it is closed. The images in that room can no longer hurt you. Do you understand?"

"Yes."

"Now Lizzy, why does Celia want your sister?"

"So she will be the only one."

Don looked quizzically at Gabe, who only shrugged.

"The only one what?" he asked.

"No sister," she replied. "She is the only child. She wants her doll back."

Gabe thought about the strange little dirty burlap doll that Shannon clutched so tightly. Celia, it seemed, was jealous.

"Alright, now I've only got one more question for you," he said. "There is another presence in the house."

"Yes."

"Do you know who it is? Did Celia tell you who it is?"

"Yes."

"Who is it?"

"Mommy."

CHAPTER 29

GABE'S HANDS WOULD NOT STOP SHAKING as he stood outside smoking. The professor had given her a suggestion to let her sleep a bit longer, and remember only what Celia really was, but nothing more. Still, Gabe wished she'd never had to deal with a session like that.

"Don't worry," said Don, patting him on the back. "She won't recall a thing and she'll be back to normal when she wakes up."

"Are you sure?"

"Reasonably," he said with a weak smile.

"So now what?" he asked, frustrated.

"Well," said Don cautiously. "We only know a third of the story."

"Huh?"

"There's three sides to every story my boy," he said. "Not two, but three. Your side, my side, and the truth. We've heard from Celia's side. Now, if we want to find out the truth, we have to hear the other side, then divine from both those points of view what is true."

"How do we do that?" Gabe asked, fearing he already knew the answer.

"By talking to the only other person in your house with such gifts."

"Shannon?" he asked incredulously.

"No. I have no doubt she is gifted, even beyond her sister, but you're overlooking someone. Your wife," he said gesturing into the parking lot where Trish was getting Shannon out of the car, brightly colored bags of food in one hand. As though she heard him, she looked up to where they were both looking down on her.

"What?" she said.

THE STAIRCASE IN HER MIND'S EYE was black, made of rough wood. It creaked when she pressed weight on each of its steps. Though it appeared odd, she didn't find it bothersome that there were no walls on either side, nor a discernable ceiling. All she could see was a dim outline of the door at the bottom of the stairs, a door that became more substantial with each step down.

Deeper and deeper said the far-away guiding voice in her mind, matching its rhythm with her own motions.

When she reached the bottom of the stairs, she turned toward the direction she had come from. The point of her origin was not clear, however, as the stairs seemed to continue up beyond her rage of vision. She turned back toward the door. It appeared ordinary enough, gray with no features to speak of. The small brass knob was scratched as though by years of use.

Open the door

She felt the knob give in her hand and as the door slowly swung open, she was bathed in brilliant light from the other side. Squinting, she stepped through into memory.

You are only an observer

She watched as her own head popped up into the relative darkness of the attic, flashlight in hand, to search for some intruder. As the Trish that wasn't her played the light around the room, the Trish that was noticed swirling motes take human shape in the rocking chair that sat in front of the dormer. She watched impassively as the Trish that wasn't opened her mouth to scream but had no time to release one as the mote-person leaped from the rocking chair and straight into her open mouth. She watched as the Trish that wasn't her fell to her knees and writhed on the floor.

What did she see?

Her perception shifted as she could feel herself drawn into the mind of the Trish that wasn't her. There, three became one as the being of dust, Hester, replayed the events of her life and death. Trish could feel the wrenching sorrow at the death of her husband, the guilt over hiding the truth. She felt the revulsion at finding what her daughter had done to any animal that happened too close to the house. She felt the fear of what her daughter was becoming.

She watched as her own hands set flame to draperies and furniture. She felt the deep pain climbing the stairs to the attic. She could hear the bitter screams of the child Celia, smell the light scent of oleander that permeated the kerosene. She could feel the burning pain where the child had stabbed her. She heard herself laugh as she clutched the familiar burlap doll close to her breast. She felt herself die in agony, quietly reserved and happy that what she was doing was right.

Return!

The voice was as a gnat buzzing in her ear. She couldn't leave. She didn't want to. She had to make sure her daughter could not commit atrocities again.

Return!

She saw the remaining timbers, breathing stickily with the evil left within them, built upon by those that had become strangers. She watched as people were driven away from the house, and how many had nearly lost their lives.

Return!

Her perception was roughly torn away from the others. She saw the Trish that was not her and Hester standing, as if superimposed on each other, in the attic as she backed quickly away from them. She felt herself pass back through the doorway and up the stairway that hung in space and consciousness. She sat up, eyes open, and sobbed openly into her hands.

Don looked to Gabe whose face was a mixture of pain and wonder. Trish had been in a deep trance, one he had almost been unable to bring her out of. The gamble had paid off, however. They now knew what, or more accurately who, was in the house. They knew why they were there, and Don, for one, had a pretty good idea of what to do about it.

His head throbbed from the concentration he had exerted during the session. He felt as if his eyes were being pushed from their sockets from the inside. He pulled a handkerchief from his pocket and dabbed at his forehead then his nose, finding the markings of blood he figured would be there.

"I have to go," he announced hastily. "But I'll be back."

"Where are you going?" Gabe stammered.

"I have to gather equipment, data, my research team..."

"What are you going to do?"

"We're going to get your house back," he replied as though it were the easiest thing in the world. "Now please, stay here and rest. I'll be back soon, then we'll go back."

"All of us?" asked Trish, glancing at the children.

"Oh, I don't think we'll need to involve the children in this," he said, patting her hand. "This is too dangerous to put them through. Is there someone you can leave them with?"

"Gabe's brother," she nodded.

"Good. Make the arrangements. I'll be back soon."

With a flourish of his hand he was gone, taking the stairs as quickly as he could without doing more damage than had already been done.

By the time he reached the bottom, the throbbing in his head had become a brutal pounding that seemed to threaten to crack his skull like an egg. He slid into the driver's seat of his car, fumbled for a moment with the keys, and then drove carefully out of the parking lot for home and rest.

Inside the hotel room, Gabe held his family closely to him, as though letting them go would give them a chance to escape the life he'd made for them. Again, depression and doubt crept into his mind, reminding him somehow, this was all his fault. Somehow, he believed, had he made better choices, had he gotten a better job, had he continued with his education, none of this would have happened.

"I'm so sorry," he said, his voice cracking as he choked back a sob.

"For what?" asked Trish as she pulled her head back slightly.

"For everything. I'm sorry I dragged everyone into this. I'm sorry I couldn't afford to keep us out of bankruptcy. I'm sorry the house I chose is killing us. I'm so sorry I didn't listen to you. I'm sorry I didn't believe."

"Honey," said Trish as she sniffed away her tears. "I wouldn't have believed it either. None of this is your fault. This family is a partnership. We did this. We brought ourselves to this. It wasn't just you. Losing my job didn't help."

"Daddy," Lizzy broke in, "don't be sad. We all love you. We don't blame you for any of this. I should have told you about Celia when I first saw her."

He couldn't raise his eyes. Through their protestations, the tiny voice inside of him still told him it was his fault. It wasn't until Shannon crawled into his lap, lifted his head, and smiled that the voice went away. She wrapped her arms around his neck and hugged him sweetly, followed by Lizzy and finally Trish, who embraced them all.

"I love you guys," he said through tears.

CHAPTER 30

THE DRIVE BACK TO HIS APARTMENT was treacherous for Don, as the migraine that hammered his head made it difficult to see, much less drive. He knew he should have stayed, slept until the pain had gone away, but he couldn't bring himself to show weakness in front of his friend and his family. They were counting on him, he reasoned, and could only see him as strong. If he showed the slightest amount of frailty, they would begin to doubt, and doubt could kill them all. He wasn't about to let that happen.

Pulling into his parking space, he noticed with growing frustration that his vision was beginning to completely darken in his right eye. As quickly as he dared, he raced up the stairwell and into his modest flat, taking only the smallest amount of time to lock the door behind him. He dropped what belongings he had with him by the door and went to his bed where he collapsed in pain. Aspirin, he knew, wouldn't help him in this state. The only thing that could dull the pain and make it eventually stop was sleep. He rolled to his back and began a low mantra, forcing himself to drift into sleep.

When he finally awoke, some two or so hours later, his head felt sore, but no longer hurt with the same violence it had earlier. This type of pain he could deal with using aspirin. He took two out of the bottle he kept on his night table and chewed them, ignoring the taste, and then got up and went to his desk. Inside the third drawer on the right was his notebook.

The small black binder was well worn with pages falling out from frequent use. Its cover was torn in several places, and many of the pages inside would have escaped had it not been for the giant green rubber band that held the book shut.

Don pulled the band off and began searching through the telephone numbers and names contained therein. He had spent much of his professional career trying to find people who were like-minded, who did not shun the paranormal, but rather, embraced it. While there were many on the list that turned out to be either charlatans or incompetent, there were the trusted few on whom he knew he could rely.

As he thumbed through the listings he tried to formulate exactly what he would say to his colleagues once he called them. Rather, there was one person in particular he wanted to convince. Though she'd told him she would never go back into that house again, Elenor's talent as a psychic medium was beyond compare.

All the scientists in the world could go to a site as overrun with power as the house on Blanco Street, but without someone who could touch the other side, they would be unable to do more than measure cold spots and die.

Elenor had the best chance of any of them of laying the presences to rest. It was up to Don to present her with enough facts that she would feel that going back to the house would be a good idea.

Through their recount while under hypnosis, Don was able to piece together what was actually happening in the house. There were two presences, of that he was certain. Both presences wanted the house emptied, but for different reasons. The girl, Celia, wanted Gabe gone, through any means necessary, and seemed to be trying to possess Lizzy, though for what reason Don could not be sure. He was certain, however, that whatever the reason, it was not good.

The other presence, the mother, presented more of a mystery to him. Through his research, he'd learned relatively little about the woman who burned her house down. The general impression he'd gotten was that she was quite mad. From what he'd heard from Trish, however, perhaps madness was not the right word. If this creature had been a murderous person in life, then why, he wondered, would it not have killed Trish the first chance it got in the attic? Why did it protect young Shannon?

As he dialed the number, he steeled himself for what was to come. He would explain to her that the family needed her and, if necessary, plead with her to come back. He knew he had no right to request this of her, as she, above all other people, was vulnerable to the presences in the house. The line rang.

"Hello?" came Elenor's voice.

"Nell, it's Don," he began. "Listen, I…"

"Don't try to stop me, Don," she broke in. "I have to go back to the house."

Don sat in stunned silence.

"They need me," she continued. "The family and spirits of the house need me. Oh Don, if you could feel what I felt when I was there last time. There's a rage and pain in that house that defies description. And that family, where did they come from? The little girls… what were their names again? They shine so brightly. If I don't get in there, I'm not sure what will happen."

"What happened to 'You can't make me go back in?'" he asked.

"I was scared," she said. "Something in that house touched me and I didn't like it, so I ran. At the time I couldn't handle it, but I can still feel it like a rock in my shoe. If I don't go back I'll never be able to get rid of this feeling."

"You're sure?"

"I'm sure."

"You know what kind of power you're in for, right?"

"I know." There was a sadness of finality to her voice.

"Alright then. I'll let them know."

"One more thing, Don," she added before he hung up. "Just you, me and the family. No one else."

"Why?" he asked with genuine surprise.

"We are the only one's involved," she said. "And it has to stay that way. The rage in this house is like a cancer. It spreads to the people it comes in contact with. We can't give it any more energy to feed off of."

"But what about documentation? Or research assistants? Or..."

"No one else," she said sternly and hung up the telephone.

Well, that was easy, thought Don as he set the receiver into its cradle, but now there was something else that worried him besides the residual pain in his head. For as long as he'd known Elenor, she'd always been the voice of caution. It wasn't like her to be so strong-headed about rushing into such a potentially dangerous situation. There had always been safety measures taken, technicians monitoring her heart rate, controls to allow her to pull away from the other side should she need. But now there was an almost reckless abandon in how she'd insisted they go back.

He set to work gathering the equipment he would need for such a job, beginning with the large aluminum case which contained detection equipment. He'd made it his habit to prepare for every contingency, so in addition to his usual equipment of a Gaussmeter, flashlight, and an infra-red thermometer, he added a small cassette recorder and two disposable cameras. He packed a general first-aid kit, a notebook with charcoal, and several chemical glow sticks. As he tucked them all away in the case, he wondered if he was truly prepared.

He'd investigated several hauntings across the country, most of which turned out to have natural origins. Some had yielded real evidence of paranormal activity, but this was the first time he'd encountered a haunting of this magnitude, and the thought excited him. Though it was true he was apprehensive, his intrigue far outweighed any fear. He took two more of the analgesics and tucked the bottle in his pocket as he picked up his case and went out the door.

By the time he arrived at Elenor's home, she was sitting outside on the steps, dressed comfortably in black baggy pants with two shirts, waiting for him. She got up quickly and briskly got into the car.

"Thanks for..." he began, only to be cut off by Elenor.

"Don't thank me," she spat. "This is all your fault. You're the one who took me to that goddamn house to begin with. If it weren't for you, I wouldn't feel this way."

"I'm sorry," he replied. "We need to pick up Gabe and Trish and we'll be on our way."

"And the children too."

"The children? Out of the question! It's too dangerous for them!" The very idea she would endanger the lives of Shannon and Lizzy perplexed and infuriated him.

"They have to come," she said sternly. "It's their energies that these beings are keyed to. The oldest one will never be rid of them unless she can reclaim her energy from them."

"But their just children!" he stammered.

"Those 'just children' are two of the most powerful of their kind I've ever come in contact with. If anything, they might wind up having to protect us."

The heated argument continued in earnest, but by the time they reached the hotel where the family was waiting, Don sat in quiet and dejected concession. He admitted he had no way of knowing what was in store for them, and that Elenor knew better how to deal with such problems than he, but he still did not like putting the children in harm's way.

As they got out of the car, they saw the family standing on the walkway, Gabe holding Lizzy, Trish holding Shannon.

"Fine," said Don to Elenor. "You tell them, because I'm sure not going to."

CHAPTER 31

"You can't be serious," said Gabe as they sat staring with gaping mouths and wide eyes at the young medium. "There is no way we're taking our kids back inside that house."

Elenor sat across from them on the second bed.

"I'm sorry to ask you to do this," she said. "I would never put anyone, let alone a child, at risk. But your children are the reason these presences are as strong as they are. They've been feeding off of the girls' energy, and they have to reclaim it if we're going to lay these presences to rest."

"But..." stammered Trish. "They're just children!"

"They're not going!" echoed Gabe.

"I'm sorry," said Elenor flatly. "They have to. Please understand. Your children are the reason these beings have as much power as they do. Celia has already bonded with Lizzy because of her talent. The only hope we have of laying her spirit to rest is for Lizzy to actively fight that bond and take back all the energy Celia has taken from her."

She paused, scanning their faces for some signs of recognition, but found only confusion in its place.

"Haven't you noticed your children are gifted? Haven't you ever noticed that Lizzy is remarkably perceptive, or that she knows what you are feeling without being told?"

It was true, they realized, Lizzy had always seemed to know when they were feeling at odds. It was as though she was eavesdropping on their thoughts. It was also damned hard to surprise her. Many times they'd planned something special, either for her birthday or for other reasons, only to have her guess what it was.

"Okay," said Gabe slowly. "But why Shannon?"

Elenor took a deep breath and looked at the toddler who smiled back at her.

"Shannon..." she began. She searched for the right words to make the parents understand. It was as though what she wanted to say would not translate into mere words. "Shannon is, perhaps, the key to everything. Everyone has some psychic ability. But what she has, I suspect, goes far beyond anything I've ever encountered. Where people like me are like candles, she's as bright as a sun. She shines brighter than anyone I've ever known, and she's only two!"

"All the more reason for her to stay the hell away from that house," said Gabe.

She turned a pleading eye toward Don, who shrugged.

"This is your argument," he said.

Exasperated, she turned back to the family.

"Alright," she said, defeated. "We'll go without her. I don't know if we can clean the house without her, but we'll try."

"No."

All four adults and Lizzy turned, startled to see a look of anger on Shannon's little face. Where she had been sitting peacefully before, she was now obviously perturbed at the thought of being left behind.

"Shannon go bye-bye," she said sternly.

Had the situation not been so grave, they all would have laughed out loud at the insistence of the child. But now, given the circumstances, her protestations lent a surreal air to the room.

"Honey," said Trish when she'd found her tongue again. "No bye-bye."

"Shannon go bye-bye," she said again. "See lady."

"Hester," said Don under his breath.

They watched as the little girl slid off the bed and waddled to Elenor and grabbed her skirt. She looked up at the medium with cheerful eyes and smiled.

"Shannon go bye-bye."

"Then it's settled," she said, moving toward the door. "Oh, bring the cat."

"Why?" yelped Lizzy, hugging Bishop tight against her.

Elenor crouched in front of Lizzy and stroked the fluffy white cat's head.

"Lizzy," she said gently. "Animals are more sensitive to spirit presences than humans. It's their basic nature to live instinctually, and that makes them more attune to what's going on around them. Do you understand?"

She nodded. "I still don't see why my kitty has to go back. He could get hurt."

"Actually, he could keep us from getting hurt. He needs to go back because he can see the ghosts before we can. He can help protect us." She stood up, but seeing the doubt still on Lizzy's face, added, "I'm no going to let anything happen to him."

Lizzy still seemed unsure, and hugged her cat snugly, but nodded her head and agreed to take him with them.

By the time they arrived at the house, it was already dusk. Don had tried to prevail upon Elenor to wait until morning, but she insisted they go that instant. While he knew there was no truth to the old stereotype that hauntings became more powerful at night, the darkness presented other difficulties, not the least of which was the creeping feeling that worked its way up and down his spine.

As the two cars pulled into the unpaved driveway, Gabe could not help but regard his youngest daughter with apprehension. She was the same as she had been every other day of his life, he knew, but he'd not seen this side of her before. As though she could read his thoughts, she turned to him and grinned.

"S'okay Daddy," she beamed.

They got out of their respective vehicles and gathered outside the gate, staring at the house as though any moment it would grow fangs, leap from its foundation and dash them all to bits.

"I'm scared, Daddy," said Lizzy as she gripped his hand tightly. He looked down at her and managed a weak smile.

"Me too, sweetheart," he replied. "But we'll get through this."

"Together," said Trish, squeezing his other hand.

"I hope so," said Elenor from behind them. She moved in front of them and crouched in front of Lizzy and Shannon. "I'm not going to lie to you," she said. "This is going to be very scary. Just hold on to each other and keep your wits about you and we can beat them. Whatever you do, don't let them back into your mind."

Lizzy nodded stiffly. Shannon grinned and took Elenor's hand in hers. Elenor straightened and looked soberly into the eyes of the parents.

"Try not to be afraid," she said. "I know how stupid that sounds, but do try. Spirit energies feed off of strong negative emotional energies. The more afraid or angry you get, the more powerful they, and weaker you, become."

"So how are we going to fight this thing?" asked Trish.

"Together," replied Don trying his best to be reassuring. His words came out hollow.

The old professor opened the trunk of his car and pulled out a photographer's vest. After donning the vest, he opened the steel case and began loading his pockets with its contents. When he was satisfied he had everything he needed, he took his place behind the group and nodded silently to Elenor. She took a deep breath and opened the gate.

As they went down the cement steps, the pungent scent of rot was in the air, coming from the stone planters. One had contained flowers, but now was full to its brim with black sludge. Vegetables had been planted in another, only now they lay decomposing on the vines, their husks withered and dark. The earth with which they were filled seemed to squirm with carrion life.

They stared, transfixed by a morbid sense of curiosity until the flash from one of Don's cameras temporarily blinded them and brought them back to their senses.

"What the hell are you doing?" hissed Elenor.

"Recording evidence," he said bluntly. "You do remember proper scientific method, don't you?"

She snorted as she turned back toward the house then stopped in her tracks. Gabe could see nothing extraordinary about the house at the moment, but Elenor seemed terrified, all of her forceful will gone. He glanced at the rest of the group to see her expression mirrored in each of their faces, save that of Don, who was busily taking readings with his meters.

He felt his stomach knot in anger and fear. For a moment, he wondered just what they thought they were doing. It was just a house, and if ghosts wanted it so badly, they could damned well have it. But no, he thought. This house was theirs. This house was the only place they had. Whether it had been a bad decision or not was now a moot point. Now the choice was either to run or fight.

It took only a moment, but the answer was clear to him. He'd had enough of running, of letting himself feel like he was incapable of providing a life for his family. He'd had enough of every decision he made turning into disaster in his hands. There would be no more running. There would be no more circumstances that forced him to swallow his pride and self-worth. This time he was determined to fight for his family. He was determined to fight for his own self esteem.

He stepped forward and in one defiant gesture, opened the door. The air was still within the house. The darkness seemed to thicken as he stood looking at it. He didn't care now. He was not angry, nor was he frightened. Now grim determination filled his heart as he stepped across the threshold and into the waiting darkness.

"Stay together," he said as he strained to see through the inky curtain. He turned when he heard no answer and realized he was alone.

CHAPTER 32

Lizzy shivered in the cold and dampness that surrounded her. She recognized the basement, but could not figure how she had gotten here. She stepped through the doorway off the terra-cotta patio, but instead of the concrete floor and sheetrock walls of the kitchen, she found herself amid the bare timbers and dirt floor beneath the house, her cat still hugged tightly in her arms.

"How did we get down here?" she wondered aloud to Bishop, who responded with a hiss toward the darkness that seemed to engulf the far end of the room. He didn't struggle or try to leap from her arms, but he twitched and spit a warning at the unseen presence, which Lizzy could feel in her stomach like a gnawing hunger.

Lizzy, she heard a thousand whispers say. *Come and see.*

Without really knowing why, she stepped forward, toward the part of the basement under the great front porch, the part of the basement that was little more than dirt and rubble.

"Celia?" she asked, her voice barely above a whisper. "Where are you?"

Here, replied the whispers in her mind. *I want to show you.*

Bishop exploded from her grasp and stood in front of her, his back arched and every hair on end. He spat into the darkness, protective of his mistress.

"They told me you were bad," she said, her voice a mix of anger and hurt. "You lied to me. You tried to hurt me."

I would never hurt you. They lied.

She could feel the words digging into her mind. Maybe they were wrong about her friend. Adults were often wrong. Maybe they just didn't understand.

But you do, whispered the voices. *You know what it's like to be misunderstood, to be pushed aside, to be ignored.*

She did understand. For some time now, it seemed her parents didn't understand who she was anymore. They still wanted her to be the child with no cares who would blindly do what she was told. But she wanted to do things herself now. She was practically a teenager and could make her own decisions.

She also understood how it felt to be pushed aside and ignored all together. Ever since Shannon had been born, her parents had admonished her for being too noisy. Most of her toys had become fodder for her little sister's destructive habits. Daddy never carried her anymore, always carrying her little sister. Mommy used to read stories to her at bedtime, but now her sister got the stories and she was told she was getting too old for such things.

She felt a cold prickle inside her as her anger toward her parents and sister grew. Of course Celia is bad, she thought, because she's my friend.

It was so much better when it was just you, wasn't it?

"Yes." She could feel herself becoming more spiteful.

It would be so much better if the other one were gone, wouldn't it?

"Yes."

You want them to hurt the way they've hurt you, don't you?

"Yes."

Come. Dig.

As she stepped toward the rubble under the porch, Bishop dropped in her path, his back arched, hissing at his young mistress.

"Get out of my way, Bishop," she growled.

He yowled deep in his throat in warning at her. Enraged, she kicked toward the cat, sending him scurrying off toward the main part of the house. For an instant, she wanted to go after him, to hold him and tell him she didn't mean it, but vengeful hatred had her now, freezing her veins.

Dig, the whispers repeated.

Lizzy knelt in the dirt and began thrusting her hands into the piles, pushing away at years of grime and soot. If she felt her flesh tear as her delicate hands dug past the rocks and clods, she didn't care.

My Daddy ignored me. He didn't understand me.

She dug deeper, feeling the words go stronger as she dug.

He wanted another, so I would not be the only one.

Deeper and deeper.

He hurt me...

Her hands, bloody from digging, found purchase on a small bundle wrapped in burlap, and inside, a lace handkerchief with an embroidered CT, buried beneath years of dirt and pain.

So I hurt him.

Lizzy unwrapped the straight razor and smiled as the blade gleamed in the darkness.

CHAPTER 33

"Trish!" he called frantically into the thickening shadows. "Lizzy! Don!" There was no answer. The darkness seemed to muffle his voice so not even his echo came back to his ears. His voice sounded strange to him, as though his head were wrapped in a towel while he shouted. He was certain they had been behind him when he entered the house, but now even the door was obscured from view by a thick darkness that seemed more like oil than air.

He reached to see if he could feel the door and jerked his hand away as cold pierced his hand as surely as an ice pick. He felt his senses race as panic began to take hold. Instinct told him to go back out the way he came, and fast, before he was trapped for good. It was, however too late, as whatever inhabited the house had covered the door and sprung its own trap. He spun, looking around the room wildly for something, anything, to try to get through the ever-thickening mess with. He picked up a stool and swung it hard, only to watch in horror as it was ripped from his hands and swallowed into darkness.

The viscous material twisted and flowed into a face that instinct told him should be all-too familiar. Its cherubic cheeks and ringlet-crowned head, the wicked curve of the lips, the cold deadness of the eyes told him immediately who was now staring him in the face. Celia.

You've failed them again, said the voices in his head. Celia's, but a choir of other voices like locusts chirping the same words, but not in unison. *You're pathetic. They don't need you anymore.*

"It's not true," Gabe tried to say, but the words would not form in his mouth. He was not aware of his feet moving backward, but without realizing what he was doing, he was running away from the face in the blackness, deeper into the house. No step was planned, his only thought to get away from the voices that pounded relentlessly at his mind.

Failure.

He was only vaguely aware that he fell, the voices in his head growing louder, gaining strength, and pounding at his psyche. His feet kicked of their own volition sending him scrambling across the carpeted dining room like a misshapen crab. He looked around the room, hoping to find some physical source of the voices, only to be met with the smoky apparition of his wife and daughters looking down upon him with disdain on their faces. Even Shannon, who offered nothing but love and happiness, seemed to look upon him with scorn in her eyes.

Look at your Father, he could hear Trish's voice amid the locusts say. *He's weak. It's all his fault we have nothing. It's his fault we came here.*

He turned away from the ethereal vision to be met by another of his mother and father.

You are such a disappointment, said the locusts with his father's voice. *You always have been.*

He's right, you know dear, echoed the locusts with his mother's voice. *You never have done anything right. You really would be better off dead.*

Gabe howled in torment as he collapsed in a heap, sobbing against a wall with the sound of a million locusts buzzing in his ears.

CHAPTER 34

DON WAS SURE THEY WERE RIGHT in front of him. He'd only glanced away for a moment to check the reading on his Gausmeter, and when he looked up, he was utterly alone, the alarm on the meter chirping wildly. The dull ache in his head began to intensify the moment he'd crossed the threshold. He ignored the ache and began searching for his missing friends.

As he crossed the kitchen, he became aware of the darkness closing in behind him, a palpable thing, and parting only a few feet in front of him at a time. It was letting him in, he realized. He had his doubts as to whether or not it would let him out.

Through the curtain of black he heard, or thought he heard, a muffled scream, a voice that sounded like Gabe's. He moved cautiously in the direction of the sound.

"Gabe?" he called out, hoping his own voice could be heard. When he heard the muffling effect of the inky blackness, he knew his own voice could not penetrate. He cursed himself for bringing the family into this. Elenor had insisted, but she and Don knew the risks involved. Gabe and his family did not. Now they were lost somewhere in the house, and though it was not an especially large structure, there were still plenty of places where they would be unable to call for help.

He turned back toward the door and watched as the dark shadows congealed into a solid mass in his path. Pulling his thermometer from his pocket, he took a reading. Whatever the mass was, it was a full 20 degrees colder than the rest of the room. He put his meters back into their respective pockets and pulled out his notebook to jot down observations and readings.

Science kept Professor Thorndyke grounded and allowed him to move through the house instead of giving in to the panic that crept into the back of his mind. Science alone kept him from trying to get out now, while there was still some chance he could escape. From his point of view, any opportunity to learn about this side of nature was a good one, although his gut told him otherwise.

The ache in his head progressed until it became a pounding, a pulse not his own, but of the house. As he continued to scribble notes, he realized his hands had begun shaking again, a sure sign the pain in his head was just beginning. It angered him that the presence, which ever one it was, had discerned his one weakness so quickly, and was now slowly tightening its grip on him, intent on debilitating him. His anger was replaced by fear when he saw a single drop of blood fall from his nose and land in his notebook.

From the corner of his vision, he thought he saw movement, for only the briefest of seconds, but he was sure he'd seen something. He advanced on the flitting image, his own vision blurring, as he moved slowly forward. With each step, the pulse in his head grew stronger, each thump a hammer in his brain.

"Hello?" he croaked. "Who's that?"

There was no answer except for giggles from the direction he was heading but could not see.

Weak old man, he heard in his head, a distant buzzing with clarity of form. *Science is your religion. A poor choice of faith.*

"You can't scare me," he said to no one in particular. "I know what you are, and you can't hurt me!"

No? asked the voice dripping venom.

As if in reply, Don's knees buckled as powerful rhythmic blows seemed to crush the top of his skull in. With each strike, he took a step backward, toward the inner part of the house. So agonizing was the pain that he didn't even realize he could not see the rest of the interior of the house.

The pounding in his head increased in intensity, and with each strike he felt sick to his stomach. As he backed away, he could feel himself reaching something not quite solid. As he turned he saw more of the dark shadow blocking his path into the house. A wall as high as the ceiling and curving inward on both sides held him fast, preventing his escape.

He put his hands to his head and clutched at his hair, eyes wide as he realized the darkness that stepped in behind him at the back door was now growing and following his movements with most dangerous intentions.

As the darkness reached out toward him with inky tentacles, the pain in his head gave way to the panic in his heart. He threw himself from one side to the other, frantically trying to avoid the cold embrace of dark hatred that oozed like a thing alive from the shadows. As he pitched to his left, he felt the sticky wall of darkness give and he fell through onto the warm carpeted floor, his senses reeling, his head still throbbing. His vision was blurred, and though he could not make any sense of what had just happened to him, he knew somehow he was granted a reprieve.

He crawled across the carpet, away from the doorway he had fallen through, leaving small pools of blood from his nose behind. He felt as though his eyes were swelling out of their sockets as he collapsed into a corner. Such power he had never felt. He wondered if this was the sort of thing mediums went through on a regular basis.

Elenor.

The thought of mediums brought Elenor to his mind with frightening clarity. Though he still could barely concentrate, he realized Elenor must be in serious danger. If the souls of this house could attack him, a non-sensitive, with such ferocity...

He didn't allow himself to finish the thought. Instead, he pulled the bottle of pain reliever from one of his many pockets, dumped a handful into his mouth and swallowed hard. It would take time for them to work, but it was all he could do at the moment.

Trying his best to ignore the pain, he pulled out his Gausmeter and flashlight. It was obviously warmer in this room than anywhere else in the house, but why, or where the heat was coming from he could not say. The pounding in his head made it difficult to read the needle, which bounced erratically across the display. He was concentrating so intently on reading the needle that when he saw something emerge from the wall beside him, he lost all composure.

"Holy Jesus Christ!" he screamed.

CHAPTER 35

THERE WAS NO SENSATION OF WEIGHT OR TOUCH, no taste, no sense of even really existing. All Elenor was aware of was darkness and pain. Rage that took decades to build welled up around her and beat down upon her in a tide of human emotion.

A new type of pain, not physical, but all the more agonizing, ripped through her being as though her mind were being flayed from the inside. Though giving in and accepting oblivion would have been easy enough, she fought with every fiber of her being.

You are not welcome here, came thousands of voices with tinkling bells. *You'll die in here. You all will.*

She focused her will and exerted her energy forward, plunging past the pain and into what was beyond: torment, suffering, sorrow.

"Who are you?" she asked in her mind as she felt fingers like knives cut into her psyche. "Why can't you rest?"

My suffering. My disgrace. My responsibility.

"Are you Celia?"

At the mention of the name, stabbing pain shot through her body and soul, jarring her focus away from the task at hand. In that instant she saw images. Blood covered walls, a razor slicing through flesh, a key locking a door.

"What does it mean?" she asked again, redoubling her efforts. "Are you Hester?"

Again, images flashed through her mind, this time not accompanied by pain. A man in a long black coat, blood flowing from his neck and chest, a strange flower, a cup of tea, a sobbing embrace from a beautiful woman with blood on her hands. Although she could not actually smell, she was aware of the thick odor of kerosene in the air and the burning sulfur as a match was lit mixed with the sweet perfume of oleander.

"Why?" she screamed in her mind. "For God's sake, why?"

My pain. My disgrace. My sorrow. My responsibility.

Elenor felt her consciousness snap back into her own mind as recognition dawned on her. She used every ounce of will she could muster and threw herself out of the nether realm. Physical sensation came back to her body as she landed hard on the wooden floor of the living room. She smiled maniacally through the pain. She knew now what the secret was. She knew why Hester had burned the house and killed her demon of a child. It wasn't because she was psychotic. It was because she was pregnant.

CHAPTER 36

Her head spun as she held tight to her youngest daughter. As they stepped through the doorway, she'd felt something pulling, as though trying to take Shannon away from her. As any mother who loved her children would, Trish held fast. Even though she'd become disoriented and had to let go of Lizzy's hand to hold Shannon, even shutting her eyes against the whirling backdrop that became her world, she held fast.

As the spinning stopped, she slowly opened her eyes to find only her youngest daughter with her. The other four people, the professor, the psychic and her beloved husband and oldest child, were nowhere to be seen. She now stood, perched precariously, on the boards that formed the floor of the attic above her room.

Before she could puzzle out the how or why of her being here, she saw the dust motes swirl and leap to life as they formed the familiar shape of Hester Tinsley. Shannon smiled as she saw the figure form.

"Hi lady!" she beamed.

Why are you here? demanded the voices of bells. *Get out!* As she spoke, Trish could feel the hot wind that had leveled her in the kitchen blowing behind the words.

"Where is my husband?" demanded Trish. "Where is my family?"

Too late, lamented the voices. *Get out now.*

"Why are you doing this?"

My shame, replied the shrinking figure. *My sorrow. My responsibility.*

As the figure came toward them, Trish could almost hear the rustling of the long heavy dress Hester wore, though it was made of dust and could make no such sound. She stood frozen on the wide beam, unable to move for fear of losing her balance and crashing through the ceiling with her child.

The dusty figure stood before them and raised a hand, gently caressing the cheek of Shannon, who giggled and snuggled against the dusty cloud. Trish felt the warmth from her hand and knew she would not try to harm her daughter.

Such a beautiful child, she heard the bells say. *Protect her, Mother. Leave this place. Leave me to my misery.*

With that, the will that held the motes of dust together was gone, leaving only a swirling cloud as the motes found new resting places.

Shannon touched her face and drew away a wet finger. Trish was unaware of the tears the wraith had brought to her eyes. So much sorrow she had never felt before. Shannon hugged her and pointed toward the open passageway that led out of the attic.

"Down," she said.

Trish nodded. "Down," she repeated as she carefully stepped on the beams to the plywood platform around the opening. It was difficult, getting them both down ladder, but through alternating climbing down and setting Shannon on a step, she finally made it back into her own bedroom. As she emerged from the opening in the wall, she caught movement out of the corner of her eye.

"Holy Jesus Christ!" shrieked the old professor as he stumbled backward, his flashlight shining at Trish and Shannon.

"Don?"

"My God!" he panted. "Where the hell did you two come from?"

"The attic," replied Trish. "We've spoken with Hester. Don, there's something wrong here."

"Oh?" He was fumbling with his flashlight. He snapped his head up suddenly. "We're in a house haunted by the ghosts of a little girl and her psychopathic mother. What could possibly be wrong here?"

"Hester wasn't crazy," she said, ignoring his sarcastic retort. "I mean she doesn't seem crazy. She seems more sad. There was a reason why she burned the house down. Something set her off, but I don't know what." She looked up at Don. "Are you alright?"

Don's hands were shaking violently and blood trickled from his nose.

"Never better," he deadpanned. "Ever since we got here, I've had the most infernal pounding in my skull. It feels like a terrible migraine. I'm trying to fight it off but..."

Shannon leaned forward in her mother's arms and pressed her hands to the sides of his face. His expression softened and the tremors stopped. As she drew her hands away, he felt the pain in his head subside and his mind clear.

"Such a remarkable little girl," he said in wonderment.

Shannon beamed back at him with the same giggling smile Trish loved so much.

"Where's everyone else?" she asked, the panic in her voice evident.

"I don't know," he replied. "I wound up alone just as you did, I suspect. I'm sure the others did too, which worries me. We're being separated, which leaves us vulnerable. We have to find the others and regroup."

"They can't have gone far," said Trish. "The house isn't that big."

"Physical laws don't seem to apply here. Besides, I don't know what you saw in the attic, but little Celia seems to be throwing a tantrum out there."

As they approached the doorway, Don took his thermometer from his pocket. If cold was the tell-tale sign Celia was present, he would like even the slightest forewarning. With the infrared beam set to its maximum distance, he could read the surface temperature of any given object up to ten feet away, as well as scan the ambient temperature of the room. While that might not give him much time to react, some was better than none. With a backward glance to Trish and Shannon, he took Trish's hand and together they stepped across the threshold into the dining area.

The dense darkness that had engulfed the room no longer held fast by the door, but was replaced with a stillness of the air. As Don waved his thermometer around, he was surprised to find the temperature normal, as though nothing had happened.

"She's gone," he said cautiously to Trish. "The cold has moved. Now where do you suppose...?"

"Gabe!"

At the sound of her voice, Don whirled around to see the cause of her concern. Curled up in a corner of the dimly lit room lay her husband, his face ashen, his entire body shaking violently. His eyes were clenched tightly closed, but that had not stopped tears from marking their path down his cheeks. As Don and Trish ran to his side, they could barely hear him babbling softly to himself.

"I'm sorry. I'm so very sorry."

"Gabe?" Trish put Shannon down and cradled her husband in her arms. "Honey? It's me. Honey? Can you hear me?"

"So very sorry..."

As they crouched next to him, they were unaware of the silent figure moving up the staircase from the basement. They did not notice the gate opening. They did not hear the hinge creak. They didn't see the pallid face of Lizzy as she crept up behind them, the straight razor glinting strangely in the half-light.

As Trish sat rocking her husband, Shannon went to him and took his face in her hands. At her touch, Gabe's tremors ceased and a hint of recognition glinted in his eyes. He threw his arms around his wife and youngest child and hugged them close, sobbing.

"It was awful," he said. "You all called me a failure. You all said it was my fault."

Trish was stunned. She'd seen him at his moodiest, when his depression drove him further into despair than she thought possible, but this was the worst she'd ever seen him. The vicious attack had been aimed where he was most vulnerable, and now she could only try to help him pick up the pieces. She felt him stiffen and gasp, then violently push her aside as he clutched Shannon to his chest and rolled into a ball.

She didn't even have time to wonder what he was doing as she saw the glinting blade slash downward, carving a perfect line into the flesh on his back from his right shoulder to his left hip. As she looked up from where she was now sitting, she saw Lizzy, a crazed look in her eyes and razor held high, being restrained by Don who was struggling for all he was worth.

"This is all your fault!" she spat at her father. "I was to be the only one! You had to go and mess everything up! You weak pathetic fool!"

Trish didn't know what to think or do. It seemed she was living in a surrealistic dream, a place she never thought could have existed, and yet there was her oldest daughter with a blade trying to kill Gabe. She felt her temper flair inside her.

She picked herself off the floor and rushed at her daughter, unconcerned with the razor, or that Don looked as if he were losing his grip, or that she might find herself slashed to ribbons. Her only thought was that the invading spirit now residing in her daughter's frame had attacked her family where they were most vulnerable. In using Lizzy as her tool, it had gone too far.

As she reached Lizzy, Don lost his grip and, with a well-placed elbow shove, was sent backward onto the floor. Trish caught her arm as it was coming down for a killing blow with the razor and hugged her tight.

"Goddamn it Lizzy, you fight!" she said through gritted teeth in her ear.

"Bitch! Whore! I'll kill you all!" Lizzy was raving now, but try as she might, she could not break her mother's embrace.

"I'm not letting you go!" Trish cried.

In the corner, Shannon wriggled out from beneath her father's gasping body to see her Mommy and Sissy locked in the deadliest of contests. She saw Don laying on the floor helpless, paralyzed by his own fear. She saw her Daddy wracked with pain, his back entirely awash in crimson. She didn't really know what or why these things were happening, only that everyone was scared and hurt.

For the first time since this entire ordeal began, she began to feel sad. She too was scared. Scared because Mommy shouted. Scared because Sissy hurt Daddy. Scared because Daddy's back was all red and sticky and he wouldn't get up. Now, sitting on the blood-stained carpet with noises in the air and her Daddy hurt, Shannon cried.

Lizzy wrenched herself backward, stealing her mother's balance and sending her face-first to the floor beside Don. With the razor held high, she leapt to where her father and sister sat. As she reached the highest point of her jump, three distinct voices cut through the air.

"No!"

Lizzy jerked backward as though she'd been shot and lay inert on the ground, the razor still in her hand, her body not even twitching.

The first voice had been Trish's own, a voice of panic. A voice full of love, both for the victims and for the assailant, but also a voice of fear of what would happen if that final slashing blow had been followed through. The thought of losing her family was more than she could bear.

Shannon's frightened and sad voice was the second. She saw her Sissy coming, but it wasn't her Sissy. It was someone else. Someone bad. All she knew was that she didn't want the bad person. She lashed out with all the will she had with the word Mommy used to stop her in her tracks.

They turned to find the source of the third voice and found Elenor, whose forceful command had combined with the other two. She stood, disheveled and angry, in the doorway of the living room. She was hurt, sore from the fall from what felt like a thousand miles up onto the hard wood floor, but she was none the worse for wear. And she knew the secret of Hester and Celia. She knew who the real monster was and why Hester had taken the monster's life along with her own. She limped to join the others.

"It isn't Lizzy," she said crouching beside Shannon who hugged her tightly. "Celia has gotten into her mind and body and now won't get out."

"I know," said Trish grimly. "There is no part of my Lizzy that could be like that."

"Don't fool yourself," replied Elenor. "Something inside Lizzy gave Celia something to hold onto. Maybe just a small bit, but it was enough.

We have to contact Hester. I know what's going on here now. I know why Hester killed them both."

"Because she was crazy," croaked Gabe as he strained under Don's examining hand. His wounds were superficial, but hurt very badly. He'd need stitches to be sure, but he would heal nicely and without any major damage, provided he didn't die of blood loss first. "Trish, t-shirts in the second drawer of my dresser. Could you please?"

Without a word, Trish disappeared into their room, returning seconds later with an armload of old clothes which she folded into large pads for his back. Don used tape from his first aid kit to hold them in place. His wounds dressed to the best of their abilities, Gabe slipped the last of the t-shirts on over the pads, giving him a strange, humped appearance.

"What are we dealing with here, Nell?" asked Don who was obviously shaken. He took the twine from his pocket and bound Lizzy's small hands behind her back and put the straight razor in one of his many pockets while he listened.

"Hester wasn't crazy. At least, not at first. The real monster here was Celia."

"You'll get no argument from me," said Gabe through clenched teeth.

"Hester was pregnant. She and her husband were expanding their family. Celia was happy being the only child and didn't want the new baby to compete with. I guess they were too busy preparing for the arrival of the new baby to pay as much attention to Celia as she wanted. She gave her mother Oleander tea..."

"I thought Oleander tea was to relax you," said Trish.

"It is, if it's diluted properly. But Oleander is also one of the deadlier poisons in nature. The poison killed the fetus, causing a spontaneous abortion. Hester didn't realize why she'd lost the baby for a while. When she found out, she was heartbroken. Her husband confronted Celia, who confessed ~ right before she slashed him to death with his own razor.

Losing her entire family drove Hester into madness. She didn't want to live with the scandal of her daughter's actions, so she burned the house down. She stayed inside so she could be sure Celia didn't get out, and because she knew the townspeople would never blame such a thing on a little girl. Better for them all to remember the little girl the way they did instead of for what she really was."

"That's horrible," said Trish.

"I know. I'm sick just being in this house."

"So what do we do about it?" asked Gabe defiantly. "This house is ours, and we're going to keep it. Now how do we get rid of these things?"

"I don't know yet. We need to contact Hester. She's the only one who knows why she's staying around and why Celia didn't go to hell like she should have."

A hot wind whipped through the room, taking them all by surprise and announcing Hester's entrance. As they watched, the ceiling seemed to glow as a bright light shone through the cracks from above and moved from the front of the house toward the bedroom where Gabe and Trish slept. In seconds, what appeared to be liquid fire flowed from the room and waved into their presence. As it stopped, it congealed and formed the familiar shape that Trish knew.

"Hester," she whispered.

She stood, burning and beautiful, in her long dress, her hair immaculately well done, her figure every bit a lady, her face one of despair. She shook her head sadly as she stood over Lizzy, and looked with pleading eyes from one person to the next.

"What does she want?" asked Gabe, tense and ready for more chaos he was sure would come.

"She needs someone to speak for her," replied Elenor. "Someone whom she knows and trusts. Someone with whom she is a kindred spirit."

"I wouldn't recommend it," said Don, holding his thermometer again in his hand. "According to this, she's over four hundred degrees. Anyone touching her is going to get burned to a crisp."

Before anyone could stop her, Trish crossed the distance between them in the space of two heartbeats. For some reason she didn't understand, she trusted Hester. She'd spoken with the ghostly mother before, and the spirit had befriended and protected her youngest daughter. Trust was a commodity in short supply recently, but Hester had earned hers.

As she embraced the figure, they all stood breathless to see the fiery creature and the lady of the house become one.

CHAPTER 37

Trish stood before them, bathed in flames, her body poised as the soul that now controlled her voice. Her very presence exuded the class and distinction of an age gone by, and though she was awash in flames and her eyes shone with sadness that decades had deepened, she was beautiful. She turned to regard each of them, taking their measure with her eyes. She stopped with her eyes on Don.

"Why are you here?" they asked, two voices combined with thousands of bells. "This doesn't concern you. Leave."

"I'm here because these are my friends, and they needed my help."

"And you?" They turned to Elenor. "What could have possibly persuaded a person such as yourself to enter a place such as this?"

"My friend asked me," she said. "So I came."

"I warned you," they said. "I tried to tell you, but you would not listen, and now my shame has taken your daughter."

"Let us help you," said Elenor. "Tell us how to put her soul to rest and yours as well."

"This is my shame," they said stiffening. "And mine alone. A lady does not lightly pawn off her responsibilities on strangers. Save yourselves and leave now."

"I won't leave without Lizzy," roared Gabe. "Please," he said softening. "Please, help us. Let us help you. Tell us how to lay her to rest. Help me get my Lizzy back."

They looked as though they were about to reply, when Shannon toddled forward, her lip turned out in a pout. Before anyone could stop her, she went to the burning ladies and held up her arms. They stooped and picked the child up, taking her into their fiery embrace. The flames engulfed her, but left her unharmed as she smiled sweetly into the eyes of fire.

"Peeeeese lady. Want sissy."

Gabe choked on his heart as he saw the features of the blazing face soften, the flames lower a bit. How she knew that the woman who held her was not entirely her mother, he would never know, but she'd made her request to Hester. She'd done this to him a thousand times, her pouty face Trish called it, and to date he could not find a way to refuse any request she made in such a manner. There was an honest love in her eyes, a genuine need that made a person want to do what she asked, no matter how ridiculous.

They waited, breathless, for what seemed like an eternity while the ladies considered. Slowly they smiled at the cherubic face and hugged her tight. The flames that covered them both lifted away like a sheet being removed and settled beside them, forming again into the shape of Hester Tinsley. She smiled to them all and then was gone as the flames of her being dissipated into the air, leaving Trish holding Shannon, who was grasping at the wisps of light as she would grab for stars.

"My God," said Trish breathlessly as the last of Hester's soul left her body. "She showed me. She told me what must be done."

CHAPTER 38

IN THE COLD DARKNESS OF THE BASEMENT a single work-light burned, casting strange shadows across the planking that formed the walls and ceiling. Although he was wounded and in a great deal of pain, Gabe dug in the rocky ground beneath Lizzy's room, the room that had belonged to Celia.

Don labored right beside him, his equipment vest lying on the ground a few meters away. He didn't care anymore about readings or proof. Whether anyone believed his story or not, his only concern was that his friend's family had been attacked, and he swore he would help put it right. With his head throbbing and blood trickling from his nose, he dug feverishly into the soil as though he were looking for treasure instead of bones. They had never found the body.

The people of San Marcos found Hester's body easily enough, but Celia was beneath rubble and soot. Instead of getting their hands dirty, they had simply left her there. The funeral was still held, with a handsome gravestone for everyone to see, but there was no body in the grave it marked.

Celia was still here, somewhere, waiting to be given a proper resting place. Until then, she remained, growing more hateful and twisted as the years passed. Hester remained as well, sinking deeper into despair, knowing she had failed, unable to leave the house until the monster that was Celia could no longer hurt anyone.

As they labored, Elenor sat cross-legged, her eyes shut, reaching out with her mind in an attempt to guide the weary diggers, as well as to detect any kind of presence that might threaten or interrupt them. Trish sat quietly humming to Shannon, who sat beside her, and to Lizzy, who lay in her lap, her hands still bound, her eyes still shut.

The temperature of the room began to drop, so gradually no one noticed.

"Mommy," said Lizzy as her eyes fluttered open. "Where am I?"

"You're home with me," said Trish as tears of joy filled her eyes.

"Why are my hands tied?" she asked, her voice full of innocence. "The string hurts my hands mommy. Could you untie them please?"

Trish dutifully reached for the knotted line only to be stopped as Bishop leapt from the beams above and landed squarely on his young misteress' chest, hissing at Trish. She drew her hand back as though the spitting cat had bit her.

"He's only protecting me mommy," Lizzy continued with a calm voice. "Untie me so he can see you're not trying to hurt me."

She reached again, only to be stopped by Shannon who clutched her arm in both of hers and held tight, her eyes wide in warning to her mother.

"That's not Lizzy," said Elenor, breaking her meditation. "It's Celia." She snapped her head toward Don and Gabe, who had stopped work at the sound of Lizzy's voice. "Dig! Hurry! You must be getting close."

"Mommy, the strings are hurting me. You don't want me to hurt, do you? Don't you love me, Mommy?"

Her words plucked at Trish's heart like birds tearing at carrion. Trish so wanted to believe her daughter. But there was Shannon and Elenor stopping her. Who was Elenor to her anyway? She'd only met her once before. How could she possibly know if it was Lizzy or not? Don claimed she was psychic, but what did that mean? There are charlatans on every channel of television every night claiming to be psychic. And what of Shannon's protestations? She was only two, what could she possibly know?

"Don't you love me anymore, Mommy?"

She drew her hand back from the tangle mass of string around her daughter's hands with tears in her eyes.

"I love you, Lizzy," she said. "But you're not Lizzy."

The sweet smile twisted into a mask of rage as Celia thrashed wildly in the little girl's body.

"You don't love her!" screamed the child as her voice broke into the wings of locusts. "I'm the only one who really loves her! None of you will leave here!"

The diggers paused in their labors as the house began to tremble around them. No fault line was to blame this time. The timbers shook with the soul's rage as surely as it was shaking the child's body. Turning back to their task, they quickly realized the rocky soil would not come easy for a shovel. Better to work by hand.

As they tossed their digging tools aside, the air was pierced by the sickening creak of wood twisting upon itself. They looked up in time to see the timbers and tiles collapse in on them, burying them in a shower of splinters and glass. The creature that was not Lizzy cackled at the worried expressions on Trish and Elenor's faces as they leapt to pull the rubble off the diggers.

As the psychic and the mother both went to help, Shannon was left alone with the wild-eyed girl who no longer even resembled her sister. In the second it took for them to realize she was left in harms way, Celia had risen and darted to Don's tool vest, rifled through the pockets, and found what she was looking for.

The razor was cool and sharp and felt like an old friend in her hands. She used its blade to cut the twine, not caring that she'd done considerable damage to her host's wrists in the process.

She turned on the frightened toddler with wicked intent in her eyes and raised her bloody hands high above her head in anticipation of the killing strike that would make her again the only child.

As the blade began the downward stroke, she felt the pain of cracking ribs as Gabe, now free of the debris, rammed his shoulder into her, taking her down at the waist. They landed roughly on dirt and cement, reopening the ghastly wound on his back. He didn't seem to notice the tearing flesh or the rush of warmth as he was busy trying to avoid the flashing razor which Lizzy swung at him repeatedly.

Her strength amazed him as the little girl fought with the power of someone twice her size, nearly overcoming Gabe several times. She swung the weapon at him, opening fresh shallow tracks in his hands and face. He knew it wasn't his daughter, but the torrent of venom that spewed from her face infuriated him more.

"You did this! You brought us here! Failure! Coward! Weakling!"

He managed to flip her onto her back, straddling her chest and pinning her arms above her head, the razor sent flying. Her face contorted in rage as she continued to spit curses at him. For the briefest of moments, he felt her, Celia, clawing at his mind.

The twisted face he saw was no longer his daughter's, but his tormentor's. He felt rage well inside him like a torrent as she struggled for her freedom. He reached behind him with his free hand and found a rock that fit his palm perfectly. In that moment of fury, he raised his bloody hand high with the intent of crushing her skull and ending the nightmare once and for all.

"Stop! You'll kill her!" shrieked Trish, unable to move to stop the deathblow.

"Daddy!" said the face below him, eyes wide and full of tears. "Daddy don't hurt me!"

He let the rock slip from his hand as the realization of what he had almost done sunk in. He was repulsed by the thoughts that had been in his mind, as though they were someone else's. He stared into Lizzy's eyes as voices buzzed like gnats in his ears. It wasn't that he couldn't hear the warnings of Trish and Elenor, but that he could only think of his angel that he'd almost hurt. He leaned forward and took her in an exhausted embrace and sobbed softly into her ear.

"I'm sorry. I'm so very very sorry," he said.

"That's not Lizzy!" screamed Trish, so loud this time that he managed to catch the tiniest bit of what she said, but too late. She wrapped her arms around him, digging her fingers into his back and biting him hard in the shoulder. He screamed in pain and fury as he managed to pull himself away and, taking her throat in his hand, he chambered his fist to strike the grinning blood-soaked smile.

"I found it!" cut Don's voice through the din. Everyone stopped what they were doing, as though his voice had somehow put their life-forces on hold. He'd managed, with the help of Trish and Elenor to loose himself from the tar-like darkness and debris, and while they fought, he had dug with his hands into the rocky earth, searching for the prize that could end this madness. The rocks split the skin of his fingers but he continued digging until he struck something hard. Prizing it loose from the earth, he held it aloft for them to see. Celia's blackened skull.

Upon seeing the bones, Lizzy began to scream and thrash wildly, throwing Gabe off her with such force that he landed in a heap several yards away. The tendrils of cold, almost liquid shadow about the room retreated back into the timbers, or fell, as though their life force were cut in the middle, and splashed like water onto the dirt and concrete floor.

Lizzy convulsed and shook, her eyes rolled so that only the whites could be seen as her head and body pitched in opposite directions. They stared in disbelief as Shannon crawled to her sister's side and placed her hand on her blood and sweat-covered forehead.

"Sissy, wake up," she said softly, her tiny voice full of fear.

Her tremors ceased and Lizzy lay limp on the ground, her head turned aside as black sludge flowed from her mouth, nose and ears. It made a sickening sound as it sucked itself from her lungs and was expelled onto the floor where it seemed to soak into the dirt and concrete. Lizzy lay coughing and gagging, her body fighting to get the last of the infection out. At long last, she sat up sobbing.

"Sissy!" beamed Shannon as the tear stained face turned to hers. Lizzy could not say anything as she wrapped her arms around her sister and hugged her close. She knew she came but a breath from losing her precious light forever, if not for her father. She spun around searching, her gaze finally falling on Gabe's tired and blood caked face.

"Daddy!" she wailed. "I'm so sorry. I didn't mean…"

Gabe took her in his arms and hugged her tight.

"It's okay," he said as Trish and Shannon joined him. Together they stayed on the dirt and concrete floor, a family, sobbing and reminding themselves of how much they loved each other.

After a bit they relaxed and sat back to survey the damage they'd all inflicted. Shannon seemed untouched by all the night's happenings, but only time would tell the psychological damage that may have been done. Trish was dirty and bruised, but otherwise unharmed. Lizzy bled from the wrists, something a hospital would surely have to look at soon, and her mouth was caked in blood. The pain in her side each time she took a breath told her that her ribcage had been damaged, a thing for which she was grateful.

It was Gabe who'd suffered the worst of the attacks. The back of his shirt was crimson from the collar to the tail. Both his hands would need bandaging, if not stitching, and his face bore several small lines that bled profusely. Once his adrenaline wore off, he would be in serious pain. He would need the hospital worse than any of them. The amount of blood he'd lost over the course of the evening was nearing lethal levels.

Lizzy was startled by the sudden presence of Bishop, who seemed to just appear at the edge of their circle. He mewed and cocked his fluffy head sideways, as though not sure yet if Lizzy were herself again.

"Bishop!" she cried, holding her arms out to the curious feline. At the sound of her voice, he leaped into her arms and purred loudly.

"I love you, kitty," she said softly.

"I'm sorry to interrupt," broke in Elenor. "But this isn't over yet."

The family stared, fearful of what was still to come.

"What do you mean, 'not over yet?' asked Gabe.

"To lay the soul to rest permanently, the body must be laid to rest," she explained. "Also, for Hester to be at rest, the truth must be told."

"NO!" The thunderous voice came without warning, sending the family scrambling away from Trish who was again bathed in flames. The air around her was hot as the flames grew larger and more intense with her anger.

"The truth must never be told! I'll not have the people think ill of my baby! Better they think me insane than my daughter a monster!"

Gabe held his children close to him, fearful of what would come. They'd just fought off one spirit. Did they have the strength to fight another, particularly one so powerful?

"Aren't you lonely, Hester?" Elenor's voice was soft and soothing over the hot wind that blew from Trish's body. "Don't you miss Cyrus?"

The flames softened around her body as Trish's face dropped, her eyes on the floor.

"I do."

"He's waiting for you. I'm sure he misses you too."

"But my child..."

"Your child," said Elenor quickly, "is also waiting for you. Your child that Celia murdered while she was still in your womb."

"But what of Celia?"

"Hasn't this gone on long enough?" asked Don, emerging from the pit. "Haven't you suffered enough? When are you going to let go? When are you going to acknowledge this was not your fault?"

His last question struck a familiar chord with Gabe. When indeed? They were kindred spirits of a sort, he and Hester. Neither of them could release control of their lives. Neither could accept that some things were beyond their control. In that moment, he felt a great swell of pity for the fiery soul, and a moment of clarity for his own being. He stepped toward his wife's body, keeping the children behind him.

"Let it go," he said softly. "None of this is your fault. I know how you feel. I'm the same way, but now that I see you... You didn't want Celia to do what she did. You didn't tell her to murder your family. She did those things, not you. It was not your fault."

The flames died down more, leaving Trish more bathed in an orange glow and less of a fiery maelstrom. She looked at him with longing in her eyes, loneliness of decades gone by. Her soul was tired of bearing the burden she had shouldered for so long.

"This house," said Elenor. "Remember when you first moved to this city, and what this house meant to you. This house was to be where your family grew. This house was to be your future, a new beginning for you with you husband and children by your side. Let this family have the love and new beginning that you did not."

The glowing figure that was Trish nodded, and for a moment it seemed Trish herself was speaking directly to the soul inside her, gently pleading for compliance. The warmth of the room shifted into a gentle, comfortable wind as Hester looked Heavenward and smiled. The glowing veil lifted from Trish's body and she gently slumped to the floor. For only an instant, the glowing mass hung in the air, pulsing with energy that radiated to everyone in the basement, and then it was gone, leaving only the tinkling of bells and a feeling of happiness.

"She's gone," said Elenor. They turned to look at her and found tears streaming down her cheeks. "I felt her before she went. I felt them all. You touched her, Gabe. You allowed her to release her hold on this world. I'm not sure, but I think her husband and unborn child came to collect her. She's gone now. The house is clean, except for this business with the bones."

Gabe and the children helped a dazed Trish to her feet, and they once again embraced. The house was theirs.

EPILOGUE

THE GREAT HOUSE WITH WHITE PILLARS stood atop its hill, looking down over the town, with a warmth radiating from it that only comes from the people inside it. It no longer seemed quiet and sentinel-like, but was now more than a house. It was alive with joy and the shouts of laughter of children. It was welcoming. It was a home.

In the six months since the Rosewood family moved in, great care had been taken in making the house seem once again proud. Velvet bows and garlands of holly and pine wrapped the wrought-iron fence, heralding the fast-approaching Christmas holidays. The flowerbeds, though still sparse in coverings, now held the promise of life to come in the spring months.

The rails on the steep staircase were decorated in pine and holly as well, and garlands covered the rails around the newly constructed front porch. An enormous wreath hung with ribbons and bells from the front door. While one man stood on the porch awed by its beauty, the other wore an expression of satisfaction and seemed quietly pleased by his handiwork.

"You did a fine job on the porch here, son," said the older man to Gabe, stomping his foot on the new boards where Gabe had fallen through. "Fine job."

"Thanks, Dad. It means alot to me."

"Kitchen looks good too. It looked like hell when you started, but it's a fine kitchen now."

The bare sheetrock had been covered with texture and paint, a shade of blue that matched both Shannon and Lizzy's eyes. The rough cabinets had been sanded, painted white, and finished out with brass knobs with ceramic flowers in their centers. The great windows were covered with curtains of lace so the sun would not glare, but one could still see the terra-cotta patio and flowerbeds. Even the concrete floor was now covered beneath a hardwood tile that made the room seem all the more warm and alive.

"Trish calls it her dream kitchen. She said she's always wanted one this big."

They finished their cigarettes and crushed them out in the ashtray that sat on the small white folding table, then turned and went back through the stained glass door into the house. As they crossed the threshold, Gabe felt a warm sense of pride. It had taken quite a bit of work, but then, most things worth having did.

"With Trish's new job, we've been able to make the payments to you and keep doing some work on the house," said Gabe.

Trish had gone back to work in property management, making a salary that equaled his own. "It's slow going, but we'll get there. There're just a couple more things that need to be done here."

"Like what?" asked his dad.

"Well, we want to turn that craft room into a playroom for the kids, and there's still some work to be done on the roof, but it'll hold for a while."

"What are you going to do with the basement?"

Gabe shuddered slightly as he thought of going back into that room. He had not been in there for any period of time since that night six months ago. He knew eventually he would have to do something with it, but for now the memories were still too fresh. Best to let the scars heal before exposing them again. He paused by the rail beside the staircase, where Bishop was lounging.

"Oh, I dunno," he said evasively, scratching the cat's fluffy head. "Maybe we'll turn it into a billiards room. Who knows?"

They crossed the dining room and into the kitchen where the smell of turkey and hot cocoa wafted through the air. Shannon toddled after her mother, pulling her apron strings while Lizzy gathered plates and glasses to set the table. Trish, doing her best not to step on the playful little child, was putting the finishing touches on the salad and preparing to transfer the enormous meal into the next room. Nancy, Gabe's mother, helped with potholders and serving silver.

The back door banged open, heralding the arrival of Toby and his family. They all hugged and greeted while the children squealed with delight at each other. Sarah immediately bustled into the thick of things in the kitchen to help, and Toby motioned for Thomas and Gabe to follow him outside where Gabe had placed a table and a pack of dominoes. They sat down at the table to play until dinner was ready and to discuss possibilities for further improvements to the yard, all with playful jibes and warm humor.

Inside, the ladies of the house chatted while they cooked.

"I love this kitchen," said Nancy as she sliced shallots. "I wasn't sure when you bought the house if you knew how much work you were in for."

"If you only knew," said Trish with a smile. "There were quite a few... unseen problems, but we got them taken care of."

"Well I think you guys have done a great job," said Sarah with great authority. "This house used to feel so creepy, but now it seems more inviting. Of course," she added," I would have done something completely different with the decorating scheme, but it suits you."

Trish smiled at the backhanded compliment. Yes, Sarah would have done something completely different with the decor, but this house did not belong to her. She had not earned the right to call this house her own. Trish and her family had bled for this house, and fought to keep it, and she was pleased to decorate it in any way she saw fit. Sarah could keep her opinions to herself.

They finished the preparations for dinner and called the boys in from their domino game. As they came in, Lizzy ran to her father and hugged him, telling him she had filled the glasses with ice and set the table with her place by his side.

As they sat down to dinner, Gabe said a prayer, the first he'd said in many years, giving thanks for the home and their lives. Most especially, he was thankful for his family. His daughters smiled at him as he finished Grace and began the intricate dance of passing around the dishes for everyone to take their portion.

"I just don't understand some of your decor," pursued Sarah. "I mean, some of your things just don't belong where you have them. Take that thing over the door. What is that supposed to be?"

Trish smiled knowingly at the heart-shaped basket that hung over the door as some would hang a horseshoe. Off the top and sides were silk ivy leaves with a rich blue bow on the top. Inside the basket sat the strange little charred burlap doll with buttons for eyes and a smile of red yarn, keeping watch over the inhabitants of the house.

"It's our good luck charm."